# HIS INHERITED
# BRIDE

# HIS INHERITED BRIDE

BY

JACQUELINE BAIRD

*First published in Great Britain 2003*
*Large Print edition 2004*
*Harlequin Mills & Boon Limited,*
*Eton House, 18-24 Paradise Road,*
*Richmond, Surrey TW9 1SR*

© Jacqueline Baird 2003

ISBN 0 263 18076 X

*Set in Times Roman 16½ on 18 pt.*
*16-0604-57675*

*Printed and bound in Great Britain*
*by Antony Rowe Ltd, Chippenham, Wiltshire*

# CHAPTER ONE

JULIA DIEZ—Jules to her friends—glanced up at the ornate carved gargoyles that decorated the outside of the old stone building and shivered, not with cold but with nerves. She had exchanged the freezing January weather in England for mid-summer in Chile, and the temperature was a sunny eighty degrees. She had arrived in Santiago late last night, and right at this moment it was the last place she wanted to be. The land of her late father, a father she had hardly known!

She had barely slept, and, getting up at the crack of dawn, she had called her mother, Liz. Reassured she was fine, Jules had spent the past few hours in a state of nervous anticipation. Unable to eat breakfast, she had consumed numerous cups of coffee, her whole attention focused on the appointment she had to keep at twelve.

She glanced at the slim gold watch on her wrist—almost noon. Time to keep her appointment with Randolfo Carducci. The name alone was enough to make her nervous, but realistically she knew as the executor of her father's will he was her last hope.

Personally she would rather live in abject poverty than take a penny from her father's estate, she thought, straightening her slender shoulders and walking into the marble foyer of the building. But she was not prepared to risk the chances of her mother making a full recovery from her breast cancer operation for the sake of a few thousand pounds.

In Jules' mind her father owed her mum that much. It had been the age-old story. Liz, as a naive eighteen-year-old, had met and fallen madly in love with Carlos Diez at a polo match in the Cotswolds; he had been a visiting Chilean polo player and a much older man. Liz had been pregnant and married within months, and Jules, born in England, was the result. Carlos had continued on the polo circuit and when he had finally returned to take mother and baby back to his ranch in Chile, the marriage had not lasted six months.

Her mum had confided in Jules, when her own youthful engagement had broken up, that her charming husband had freely admitted he'd had a mistress in Santiago, and he'd had no intention of remaining celibate while travelling the world playing polo. Liz had returned to England with her baby. She had basically run away and a quick divorce had followed.

Jules did not blame her mum. Her own experience with her father had been a disaster. Offered a holiday in Chile at the age of fourteen, she had leapt at the chance of meeting a dad she had never seen since she was a baby, and had no memory of. Immediately she had developed an enormous crush on the neighbouring rancher's son, twenty-year-old Enrique Eiga. Encouraged by her father, she had visited Chile each summer and had been engaged at seventeen and set to marry Enrique at eighteen before she had woken up to reality and broken the whole thing off. She had never been back to Chile or spoken to her father in the seven years since, and she would not be here now if it weren't for her mother.

Reception lay through a set of wide glass doors, and she caught a glimpse of her reflection as she passed through them, and held her head a little higher. Not bad, she told herself.

Jules had opted to wear a cream knee-length linen skirt, with a loosely tailored short-sleeved linen jacket to match. She had woven her long hair into a French braid, and with the addition of fine-heeled sandals lending height to her average five feet five she thought she looked smart and businesslike.

The receptionist was a young man, and his appreciative glance swept over her as she stated her business.

'Señor Carducci is expecting you.' He smiled and added in Spanish, 'Lucky dog,' unaware Jules understood, and her lips twitched as he ushered her into an elevator adding, 'His secretary will meet you and escort you to his office suite.'

Jules said, 'Thank you,' with a smile. It never ceased to puzzle her why men seemed to find her attractive. After all, because she was a chef and with her mother ran a success-ful bakery, her figure was more lush than lean, and so she dressed to disguise the fact. Her features were even, and she had inherited her mother's pale complexion, and large, unusu-ally brilliant green eyes, but her hair revealed her mixed parentage, a dark auburn with a tendency to curl wildly unless strictly controlled.

It was a short journey, two floors, but long enough for Jules suddenly to be stricken with another attack of nerves. The elevator door slid open and she stepped into a deeply carpeted hall, and utter silence.

Jules looked around. There was no secretary in sight, and only one door as far as she could see, directly opposite the elevator. She waited, minutes passed and another glance at her watch showed it was past twelve. Was Carducci playing some kind of diabolic mind game? She wouldn't put it past him, and in a way she didn't blame him. He had called her out of the blue five months ago and proposed she reconcile with her father; three more calls had followed and she had ignored his every suggestion.

Mainly because, by an appalling coincidence, it had been at the same time as her mother had been diagnosed with breast cancer. Jules had received the first call from Randolfo Carducci the week before her mother's operation had been scheduled. A call telling her that her father had had a slight heart attack, nothing serious, he was not in hospital, but Randolfo thought Jules should maybe visit, or at least call her father. In his opinion it was time father and daughter buried their grievances and made up.

She had been so surprised at hearing a voice from the past that she had said she would try, and the call had ended amicably.

The next call had been on the eve of her mother's operation. Carducci had told her that her father had had another much more serious attack, and was hospitalised, and he had arranged a flight for her from Heathrow to Santiago at ten the following morning. The ticket was waiting for her at the airport.

Jules had abruptly turned his offer down, as she had wanted to be at her mother's side when she had her operation. The conversation had ended far from amicably. The third call had been over a week later, to inform her her father was dead, and the date of the funeral had been brutally blunt. Still Jules had declined to attend, more worried about her mother's recovery…

Jules knew how it must look to Carducci, a daughter not speaking to nor visiting her father and not turning up to his funeral! But perhaps when she explained the circumstances he would be reasonable.

Still the thought of seeing him again filled her with unease. Randolfo had been staying at the ranch when she had arrived as a teenager visiting her father for the first time. An Italian with business interests in South America, apparently he had visited the ranch the previous year at the request of his stepmother Ester. Ester was the sister of Jules' father and technically she supposed Rand was her cousin but no blood relation.

At twenty-seven he had already been a highly successful businessman, and engaged to a Chilean girl—the stunningly beautiful Maria. He had met Maria in Santiago when she had been singing in a nightclub and trying to make a name for herself in the music business. Coincidentally it had turned out that her mother had lived and worked as the cook on the Eiga ranch, next door to the Diez ranch that Randolfo visited.

To the young Jules he had seemed a different generation altogether, too uptight to be a friend—an acquaintance at best, and a disapproving adult at worst. Personally she had been unable to imagine what the young, trendy Maria had seen in him. But later she had found out…

Jules grimaced. Knowing what she knew, meeting the pompous Randolfo Carducci again was not going to be easy. Still, she would brave a lion's den for her mother, and with that thought in mind she gave up standing in the hall, 'like patience on a monument', and briskly opened the door in front of her.

A quick glance around and she realised she was still alone. The room was elegant, a mixture of soft creams and beige contrasted with deep-cushioned sofas in taupe leather, and the artwork on the walls looked genuine. The whole ambience was one of understated elegance and serious money, but the room was empty.

She walked over and sank down on one of the sofas, a sense of anticlimax making her shoulders slump dispiritedly. Geared up to do battle at twelve, she found it very deflating to be still waiting at quarter past. What now? she wondered. And looked around again.

At that moment a door opened and Jules automatically glanced across to the man who walked into the room. Randolfo Carducci...

Her eyes widened in shock, and for a moment she was stunned by the sheer masculine power of his presence. He was over six feet tall, with black hair slightly silvered at the temples and cut expertly to his arrogant head; his sculptured features were not classically handsome. Striking was a better description, with high cheekbones, a typical Roman nose that proclaimed his Italian ancestry, and a determined jaw. He was certainly the most impressive specimen of manhood she had encountered in quite a while. But then she was no expert, Jules ruefully acknowledged. She had had very little to do with men since her broken engagement. And this one was almost certainly married anyway.

The light grey suit he was wearing was tailored perfectly over broad, powerful shoulders and a white shirt open at the neck contrasted sharply with his olive-toned skin. The jacket was open and a grey leather belt supported softly pleated trousers that hugged lean hips, powerful thighs and long legs. He was awesomely male and Jules suddenly wondered how she had never noticed the fact as a teenager. As she tilted her head back her green eyes clashed with hard black, and thick arched brows came together in a frown. Nothing had changed there then, Jules thought dryly.

Jules had always felt uncomfortable around the man in the past. At thirteen years older he had seemed so commandingly superior. When he had frowned disapprovingly at her, especially when she had been with Enrique, she had felt somehow threatened.

But with hindsight she realised she had been equally disapproving of him. She had resented the easy relationship he had shared with her father, a father she had only just been beginning to know. Also his friendship with Enrique Eiga, who at the time Jules had thought was the love of her life.

Squashing the unwanted memories, she rose to her feet, and her heart gave a sudden jolt as his lips, perfectly moulded and sensuous, parted in a brief social smile. Jules shivered without knowing why... She was wrong; he had changed. He appeared even more arrogantly aloof than ever.

Stay cool, calm and in control, it is business, nothing else, Jules told herself. She had the confidence to handle any situation, and politely she held out her hand.

'Mr Carducci, nice to see you again.'

'Rand, please; after all we are almost family,' he said smoothly, his dark eyes widening speculatively on the woman before him. A lustrous mass of red hair was swept back in a braid and revealed the exquisite oval of her face. Large, thick-lashed dark green eyes looked up at him, but avoided direct contact with his. Add a small straight nose and a luscious pink mouth that begged to be kissed and the woman was dynamite! His gaze dropped lower to a hint of cleavage exposed by the vee neckline of her jacket. His body tensed. The picture of a red-headed beanpole-type teenager he had carried in his head for years blasted into oblivion by the physicality of the woman before him. Julia Diez had developed into one very sexy lady.

He watched as she looked at him, noted the flare of recognition in her brilliant eyes, and the flicker of something very like fear. She had good right to be afraid, he thought cynically, the heartless little tart. He had not seen the woman in eight years, her shape had changed, but he would have recognised those eyes anywhere.

'Sorry for the delay, Julia, my secretary should have been here. I hope you have not been waiting long.' And he grasped her still-outstretched hand.

Jules swallowed hard. His handshake was firm and warm and did very odd things to her pulse rate. 'No, not long,' she managed to respond steadily. 'And please call me Jules, everyone else does,' she said, but when she tried to pull her hand free of his he simply tightened his grip.

'Please, sit down.' Leading her back to the sofa, he waited until she sat down before freeing her hand, adding, 'It's been a long time since we met. It must have been your engagement party when you were what? Seventeen, eighteen.'

'Seventeen,' she confirmed shortly; the last thing she needed was to be reminded of her engagement party, especially not by this man. Jules hadn't seen him since, but, lifting her head, she stared at him, and for a fleeting moment she sensed something dangerous in the unfathomable black eyes and his wide-legged stance. Rand was a man to be wary of, her every instinct cried, and, remembering his fourth and final call some days after her father's funeral, she shivered slightly.

Rand Carducci had informed her with mocking cynicism evident in his tone, that he was the sole executor of her father's estate, and her father had added a codicil to his will the week before he died, the gist of it being if she agreed to return to Chile within six months of his demise she would receive something of value.

Jules had bluntly informed him she was not interested, and she had never intended taking Rand up on the offer, but now five months later she needed money. Strictly speaking it was her mother who needed the money. Her consultant had recommended a new three-year course of treatment from America as her best chance of a full recovery after her operation, but it was only available privately in England, and Liz was scheduled to start the treatment in ten days' time. Jules had assured her mother they could afford the extra expense as only the best was good enough for her beloved mum.

Jules had taken over the running of the bakery a year ago from her mum and she had embarked on an expansion scheme to provide corporate catering. At Jules' instigation they had moved from the flat above the shop, and bought a new house six months ago. The flat had been converted into another kitchen and office space with the help of a loan from the bank, plus the addition of a new catering vehicle. Unfortunately for Jules by the time the new treatment had been mentioned their finances had been stretched to the limit.

Jules had kept the information to herself, not wanting to worry her mother. She had approached the bank but they would not lend her more money so soon after the original investment, and suggested perhaps in another six months when her business plan showed a profit. Her mother could not wait six months, and Jules had tried every avenue but could not raise the cash. Finally in desperation she had contacted Rand Carducci's office in Italy. Courtesy of his secretary a flight ticket and a hotel booking had arrived two days later for Jules to travel to Chile as instructed. From the man himself she had heard not one word.

But now that she was face to face with Rand, asking what her father had left her, and demanding if whatever it was could be converted into cash, seemed a hundred times more daunting then it had yesterday.

'I was sorry to hear your engagement to Enrique did not work out.' Startled out of her troublesome thoughts by his deep, mocking voice, she tensed warily as he continued, 'I arrived at Carlos' home the day before your wedding only to discover you had called it off, according to your very disappointed father, because you thought you were too young, and you wanted to have some fun before you settled down. Rather sudden, wasn't it?'

Fun… It had been the worst time of her life and yet, according to Rand, her father had made her sound like some flighty bimbo. Her green eyes cautiously searched his, and for a second she thought she saw a flicker of some emotion in the dark depths—sympathy or censure? She wasn't sure. Did he know the real truth about her broken engagement?

'Yes, well. I had my reasons.' She lowered her long lashes, avoiding the question in his too astute gaze. It wasn't up to her to tell Rand the truth. If her late father had chosen to tell everyone it was because she had thought she was too young for marriage, so be it.

The reality was different. Three days before her marriage, when most of the household had been taking a siesta, she had been too strung up with excitement at her approaching wedding to rest. Instead she had decided to walk across to the neighbouring ranch where Enrique had lived and surprise him…

The two haciendas were situated either side of the river not a mile apart, the river being the border of the two ranches. She had crossed the water not by the bridge, but by the old stepping-stones set a few hundred yards downstream hidden by the trees.

She had only gone a few yards through the trees when she had stopped dead, and to this day she could not forget the sight that had met her eyes.

Enrique her fiancé, stark naked, with an equally naked Maria, Rand's fiancée, and completely oblivious to her presence! There was not the slightest doubt about what they had been doing, and with nausea rising in her stomach she had run away.

Jules had made it back to the other side of the river before she'd collapsed on the bank crying her eyes out. That was how Maria had found her. Jules had slapped Maria's hand away when she'd reached out to comfort her, and Maria had instantly guessed what had happened. 'You saw us.' Jules had not needed to confirm it. Maria had been able to see it in her face.

What had followed had been a painfully succinct lesson in life for Jules. Maria had informed her that she and Enrique had been lovers since the age of fourteen until her mother had found out and sent her to live in Santiago with an aunt. No one else knew of her relationship with Enrique, and no way did she want Jules revealing the truth to anyone, especially not her fiancé, Rand Carducci. He had financed her singing career and she had fully intended to marry him eventually, when she'd become tired of the music scene.

When Jules had said that was disgraceful, and if Maria married anyone it should be Enrique, because Jules certainly wasn't going to marry him now, her teenage view of love had been killed stone-dead and the very thought of Enrique touching her turned her stomach.

Maria's response had been a shake of her black head. 'God, you are such an innocent. Surely you must have realised no hot-blooded Chilean male would be content to see his girl-friend for one month a year, and even then Enrique barely kissed you. Do you really think he is marrying you for anything other than your father's ranch? Look around you—your father and Enrique's have agreed between them you will inherit this and consequently, as your husband, Enrique. Two good properties amalgamated into one great one and the two families united. Grow up, girl, and face reality. Why do you think your father waited so many years before sending for you? Because he waited until you were of an age to be used,' she told Jules cynically. 'As for Enrique, he loves me, and he would marry me tomorrow if I agreed, but no way do I want to be stuck out in the country for the rest of my life. Rand is a much better bet, and I'll get to travel the world in the lap of luxury.'

With the veil of innocence so brutally torn from her eyes Jules had been forced to face the fact that what Maria had told her made a horrible kind of sense. When they had finally parted Maria had elicited a promise from Jules that she would not mention her name in connection with Enrique.

Later Jules had told her father she was calling off the wedding because she had caught Enrique with another woman. He had told her not to be so silly, sex was not the same as the love between a married couple, and she would soon learn.

Jules had tried to argue, but had been finally silenced when her father had lost his temper and told her the truth. It had all been arranged with Señor Eiga that the two ranches would amalgamate when Jules married his son. As his only child and a female, it was her duty to do as she was told. If not he would cut her off without a penny.

It was then that she had finally seen her father for what he had been.

Remembering the episode again now still made Jules wince, mortified at her own blind innocence.

Rand saw the tightening of her full lips, but stared down at her making no effort to break the lengthening silence. He wasn't surprised Jules was lost for words with what she had on her conscience. Idly he speculated what excuse she would come up with for her callous disregard of her father, but as she continued to avoid looking at him he found his anger rising. 'I suppose you heard Enrique died in a car crash a few months later,' he prompted with barely veiled contempt.

At the sound of Rand's voice Jules blinked, banishing the hurtful memories to the back of her mind. 'Enrique's father sent me a note,' she confirmed shortly. It had arrived via a solicitor, and it had been a shock. She recalled the hatred in the short one-liner, the gist of it being that it was her fault his son was dead. Enrique had been driving recklessly because Julia had broken his heart and his father hoped she rotted in hell!

A flash of rage sparkled in Rand's black eyes. She knew about the car crash, the crash that had killed his fiancée as well as her ex, and yet she had the nerve to face him. God, she was hard, but, controlling his temper, he said, 'Even though you had parted, it must have come as quite a shock to you.'

His large hand reached and squeezed her shoulder for a moment, and Jules felt the pressure of his fingers right through to the bone. 'Yes,' she murmured, surprised by his apparent if somewhat fierce gesture of comfort.

'I am sorry. Forgive me for reminding you of your grief,' he drawled softly.

From her sitting position she felt at a distinct disadvantage, his great frame towering over her, crowding her, and, lifting her chin, she looked up into his dark face. Was that sincerity in the night-black eyes that held hers? She wasn't sure. He had the 'sorry' and the 'forgive me' in there—so why did she have the uneasy feeling she had just been insulted?

'Yes, well, thank you,' she murmured, feeling more of a hypocrite by the second, 'but I prefer not to talk about it.' She lowered her eyes from his intent gaze, her mind in a state of flux. He must know why she was here, so why was he being so *nice*? Perhaps marriage and a few children had mellowed him, she thought.

# CHAPTER TWO

THIS interview was not going at all as Jules had planned; she was not here to relive the past but to hopefully assure her mother's future. 'I did not come all this way to talk over the past. The present is more my concern,' she said firmly.

'Yes, of course, how foolish of me to think you might need sympathy. After all, you left Enrique virtually standing at the altar.' Rand stepped back and with a lift of one broad shoulder added, 'Why would you be worried about the death of an ex-fiancé, years ago, when you were not even concerned with the recent death of your own father?'

Jules' head shot back up, her green eyes clashing with contemptuous black, her doubts of his sincerity confirmed, and she realised the gloves were off with a vengeance.

'You know nothing of my relationship with my father.' She leapt to her feet. 'Or, rather lack of one,' she added cynically. 'And it really has nothing to do with you anyway.'

One of the few times Jules had had a conversation with her dad he had explained how years ago when his sister Ester had been a student she had got involved with a far left political party in Chile. After spending a term in prison for her beliefs, she had finally escaped to Europe. She had met and married an Italian widower with a four-year-old son, Randolfo, and never returned. Brother and sister held completely opposing political views, and they had been estranged for decades. Which with hindsight should have told Jules something about her dad's character years ago, but it had taken her own engagement to reveal him in his true colours.

Jules seriously doubted her father would ever have contacted his sister, if she had not made the first move years later by asking her adult stepson to check up on her only sibling on her behalf. Carlos Diez had been a cold-hearted, manipulative man as Jules had discovered for herself.

'It does have something to do with me in as much as I am the sole executor of your father's will,' Rand reminded her.

'And of course your obvious concern must be looking after your stepmother Ester's interest, I understand that,' Jules shot back throwing caution to the wind. 'But I don't—'

'Stop right there,' Rand cut in. 'I have no intention of discussing business with you on an empty stomach. Join me for lunch, and then we will talk.'

She didn't want to join him for lunch; in fact she wanted to escape from his powerful presence as soon as humanly possible. But one look at the grim determination in his darkly attractive face, and she knew she had little choice in the matter. Rand Carducci was not a man to be pushed around by anyone, and, if she was to have any chance of getting what she had come for, she could not afford to antagonise the man. 'Lunch would be nice,' Jules agreed.

Nice was not a word Rand would have used. Jules had developed into a very beautiful woman, on the outside at least, but at the moment the red tinge to her cheeks and the angry confusion in her flashing green eyes told him all he needed to know. Jules was a gold-digging, heartless little witch and she knew what side her bread was buttered on.

His firm lips twisted in a cynical smile that did not reach his eyes. He might have had some lingering sympathy for the skinny kid he remembered, but the simmering sexuality of the woman before him did not evoke sympathy, but a much more basic emotion. She was the type who could get any man she wanted with a glance from her brilliant emerald eyes and probably did. Carlos Diez apart, Jules owed him personally—if Señor Eiga was to be believed she had indirectly cost him a fiancée. A long time ago, true, but not something Rand could easily forget.

It was in his power to make sure she did not get a cent and he was sorely tempted to do just that. But he was an astute businessman, with a multimillion-dollar corporation to run, and he had neither the time nor inclination to hang around in Chile longer than was necessary. He would settle with the woman for as little as possible. There were other people more worthy who had to be considered.

'Good. I am glad you agree, and I do understand your concern over your father's estate,' Rand said smoothly, not by a flicker of an eyelash revealing the anger simmering inside him. 'And I can assure you, you will get your just reward, trust me—' cupping her elbow with one strong hand, he urged her towards the door '—but there is no great hurry. As you have taken advantage of the travel arrangements my PA arranged for you I gather you aren't planning on going anywhere for the next week,' he opined hardily. 'And it is good to see you looking so well and with the past firmly behind you.'

'Yes, well...' Was that a compliment? Or was he being sarcastic yet again? Jules wondered. But, glancing at him, she added politely, 'Thank you.' What else could she say? She needed his help.

Rand's glittering black eyes scanned her beautiful face, his strong jaw line clenching hard as he noted the evasiveness in her expressive eyes, exactly as he'd expected. When he had heard Jules had run away from her fiancé and her father, he had not been very surprised. She had seemed little more than a child to Rand when she'd got engaged, and far too immature for marriage. As for her father,

Carlos, he had been a hard man to like. If it had not been for Ester, the only mother he had ever known and adored, asking him to visit the man when he was in Chile on business, he doubted he would naturally have made friends with Carlos Diez.

Rand let go of her arm a moment and turned to lock the office door, his firm lips twisting in a dry smile. He was quite sure she would not run away from *him*; she had too much to lose, and yet for years he had not thought badly of her.

The car accident a few months after the aborted wedding had been just that, an accident, Rand had told himself at the time, and, though he had been devastated by the result, it had never entered his head to blame Jules. If anything he had felt slightly sorry for the girl. But he knew Señor Eiga had been convinced Enrique had been driving recklessly because he'd still been heartbroken over Jules, a hard-hearted young woman, and her own father had agreed with him.

Privately Rand had thought if anyone had been to blame it had been Enrique for allowing his emotions to overcome his common sense.

It was all right to be reckless with one's own life, but not with somebody else's.

Rand's opinion had begun to change when Jules had not contacted her father after he had called her to suggest she do so. Then he'd begun to wonder if the two old men had been right all along. Maybe Jules at eighteen had not been the innocent young girl he had thought. Then when she had never responded to his second call or the third, nor turned up for the funeral, he'd been virtually convinced of it, and his own anger and guilt had clicked in with a vengeance. Seeing the beautiful, sophisticated woman she had become, he was totally convinced, and any thought of trusting her was banished from his mind.

Turning, he took her arm again, his hard, chiselled features schooled into a polite, sympathetic mask. 'Your father's death must have been unsettling even though you two were estranged at the time. Grief has a way of sneaking up on one, when one least expects it,' he said softly, ushering her into the elevator.

He was right. The night of her father's funeral, alone in the house, she had cried her eyes out for the man who had given her life, recalling only the good times they had spent together. Carlos Diez had not been a bad man, Jules had finally acknowledged, simply a product of his environment, an environment totally different from the sleepy English market town she had grown up in.

'Yes,' she murmured, glancing up at him, and for a second he stared down into her brilliant green eyes, and she was suddenly aware of Rand's hand on her arm, and the warmth of his large body reaching out to envelop her, his slight masculine fragrance teasing her nostrils. It made her breath catch in her throat, and her every muscle tense. She felt her breasts swell and the sudden tightening of her nipples, something that had never happened to her before. She was so shocked by her body's treacherous reaction she shuddered, and, drawing in a deep unsteady breath, she swallowed hard. 'Yes,' she repeated.

Rand felt the slight tremor and his eyes slid astutely over her bent head, the pulse fluttering at the base of her throat, and his lips quirked at the corners in the briefest of satisfied smiles. The lovely Jules was not immune to him, he was sure. He was well aware of his effect on the opposite sex. He did not delude himself that just his face was his fortune; in his experience power and money were a much more potent aphrodisiac to the female of the species. Add a sophisticated expertise in the bedroom, and he knew without conceit he could please any woman he wanted. Not that he had bothered for quite some time, he suddenly realised.

Well, that was about to change, he decided, his eyes glinting with the thrill of the chase as they skimmed over her shapely length. The next few days promised to be very interesting, and he set about putting Jules at her ease by letting go of her arm and leaning back against the lift wall.

'I have to admit, Jules, I only visited Carlos a few times in the last eight years, mostly at the instigation of Ester, of course,' he said smoothly. 'She and my father still live in Italy and as Ester is not fit enough to undertake a long-haul flight, the unfortunate result of her imprisonment here decades ago, she also missed the funeral, but it never stopped her thinking about her only sibling.'

His mention of the funeral was deliberate, but Jules ignored his comment.

'And do you still live in Italy?' she asked. With a bit of space between them she managed to speak reasonably steadily and, glancing up, her green eyes met amused black, and his firmly chiselled lips parted over gleaming white teeth in a mocking smile, letting her know he had noted her evasion, but he answered her question.

'I visit the family home in Rome frequently, though I do have a place of my own at the coast. But my business takes me all over the world, so I have an apartment in New York, another here in Santiago, and yet another in Japan.' His smile lightened. 'Oh, and a beach house on the Gold Coast in Australia. I believe in controlling all my considerable assets personally,' he said and her gaze slid involuntarily down over his impressive body. 'I am very particular as to who I allow to check my assets.'

She would have had to be as thick as a brick not to get his very obvious *double entendre*, but even so Jules felt the tell-tale flush of colour burn up her cheeks, and was mortified when she realised where she had been looking. Plus the quite unexpected heat curling in her belly did not help. She had never felt that kind of sexual curiosity about any man... Her head jerked up. Get back to the reason you are here, girl, she admonished herself.

'Well, lucky you,' Jules blurted. 'It must be nice for you and your wife.' She reminded herself he must be married by now. Maria would never have let him get away, but she could not bring herself to say the other woman's name. 'But some of us are not so fortunate, and that is really why I am here.' At that moment the elevator doors slid open.

Rand grasped her arm again and she shot a startled glance up at him and saw the flash of rage in the depths of his eyes and tensed. 'I am not married, and you are fortunate to be alive,' he declared forcefully, then as if sensing her unease he added. 'We both are, so we should celebrate the fact,' and with an elegant shrug of his broad shoulders concluded, 'You are a long time dead, I believe is the English expression.'

She must have imagined the anger in his eyes, because he was smiling down at her, encouraging her to share his humour. 'Yes,' she murmured, still reeling from the shock of discovering he had never married Maria after all. They had been engaged for at least four years that Jules knew of.

'Come.' His hand dropped from her arm and settled in the small of her back and urged her outside to where a chauffeur-driven car waited.

In no time at all she was sitting in the back seat of a limousine with Rand at her side, and the driver was weaving the car through the midday traffic, and out into the countryside.

'Where are we going to eat?' Jules asked, the prolonged silence playing havoc with nerves strung so tightly that the tension was a frantic beat through her body. 'We seem to have left the city,' she mumbled, swallowing hard as the car took a bend and his hard-muscled thigh brushed against hers, with a resulting electric effect on her fragile control. She could not believe what was happening to her.

Normally she was the most staid of women; in fact she was still a virgin. Somehow after the fiasco of her engagement to Enrique she had gone off the idea of sex and love altogether. Yet, glancing at Rand's hard, chiselled profile, she found herself wondering what his lips would feel like on hers and tore her gaze away. But there was worse as she found herself watching his large elegant hand resting lightly on a strong thigh, and for a moment wished it were resting on hers. Where were all these crazy feelings coming from, for heaven's sake? Surely it wasn't just because she now knew he was single... She hadn't even liked him as a teenager.

'My surprise,' Rand declared, slanting her a slow, intimate smile. Her heart missed a beat and for a moment she simply stared at him. 'But I am sure you will like the place,' his deep voice drawled, soothing and seductive. 'And don't worry, we can talk seriously later.'

'Yes, b...' A long finger closed over her lips.

'Relax, and prepare yourself for a gourmet delight,' he told her. 'As long as you like fish,' he ended with a spark of rueful amusement in his tone.

'Yes.' She was fast becoming a yes-woman, Jules thought dryly. Most unlike her. But he really was a very compelling man. Strikingly attractive, add power and that aura of untouchability that only the seriously wealthy exuded, combined with one hundred per cent virile masculinity, and he was a walking aphrodisiac to any female from eight to eighty. Not a type that had ever impressed her in the past. Unfortunately for the first time in years Jules was forced to face the fact she was no exception, she conceded ruefully.

She had always thought of him as a dark, serious kind of man and yet he had a smile that she suspected could beguile any woman's heart, even hers. She gave a small involuntary shake of her head. How had she never noticed before? she wondered in amazement. Maybe because in the past he had rarely smiled at her, but that wasn't strictly true. He had on one occasion.

A memory of sitting on the paddock fence watching Enrique perform on his horse suddenly surfaced. Rand had strolled up beside her, and put a friendly arm around her waist. 'Mind you don't fall, kid,' he murmured. 'I don't want you injured before Ester has a chance to know you or she will have my guts for garters—an English expression…no?'

She laughed at his funny accent, and then he asked her if she would mind if Ester wrote to her, explaining he had told his stepmother he had met her, and Ester had never known her brother had married or had a daughter until now.

Jules glibly answered, 'Yes, fine, but I should warn you I'm not much of a letter-writer.' She turned her head to look at him; his face was only inches from her own. 'But I'll add her to my Christmas card list.' He ruffled her hair and said thanks and she recalled for a moment being dazzled by his smile, but putting it down to the bright sunshine...

The restaurant was everything Rand had said and more. A timber building set on stilts and with a long deck stretching out over the Pacific Ocean. They opted to eat outside and Jules took her seat and looked around her in awe. On the edge of a headland the sweeping view of a huge sandy beach and the sea gave the impression of being surrounded by water. 'This place is incredible.' She turned shining eyes up to Rand.

'Good, I am glad you approve. Now let me get you a drink. Champagne by way of a cel-ebration, perhaps—it has been a long time.'

One dark brow arched sardonically. 'Some might say too long'. He still found it incredible she had not turned up for her own father's funeral, and he wondered what excuse she would come up with. But he was not about to ask her. Not yet…

He had thought with each month that had passed after he had informed her of the codicil to her father's will, as she had refused point-blank to have anything to do with it, that maybe the woman had a grain of integrity after all. At least she was consistent in ignoring her father in life and death. But when Jules had contacted his office just a few weeks before the deadline on claiming any inheritance ran out, he had realised cynically her initial refusal had obviously been a ploy not to sound too eager, and make him think better of her.

Well, it hadn't worked; it simply confirmed what a hard, selfish woman she was. Carlos had maybe not been a good husband or father, but whether he had deserved a wife who had run out on him within a year of their marriage, taking his daughter with her and then divorcing him, was debatable.

To give Carlos his due, he had tried to make it up with his daughter years later by welcoming the teenage Jules into his home. When she had pleaded she was old enough to get engaged to Enrique, at the tender age of seventeen, Carlos had not objected, but had given her a big engagement party. The next year he had arranged a huge wedding at considerable expense, only to have his daughter run out on her fiancé, much the same as her mother had run out on him. In fact one could say it was Carlos Diez who had come off worse with his involvement with the English women all down the line.

Yet here this beautiful woman sat looking as cool as a cucumber, and after all she could get. Well, this time she was in for a rude awakening; Rand was going to make sure of that...

'I was sorry I couldn't make the funeral, but my mother wasn't very well.' Jules chose her words with care. She still had difficulty saying 'cancer' out loud, especially to a relative stranger. But she knew exactly what he was referring to by his 'too long'. She could recognise sarcasm when she heard it. 'And it was too short a notice to get out of an extremely important commitment I had already made.' It was the truth; she had promised to stay with her mother while she was in hospital. But she did not want to offend the man when she was hoping to get money out of him so she did not elaborate.

Never mind her mother, it was probably down to some man, Rand thought cynically. Jules had dressed down her sensational figure, but to the discerning eye she was the epitome of female pulchritude, full breasted, a tiny waist and softly rounded hips plus long, shapely legs. He stirred uncomfortably on his chair, surprised by the stirring in his groin and resenting the effect she had on him, but masking it with a fulsome compliment.

'I understand. An exquisitely beautiful young woman like you must have many more pressing calls on your time,' he drawled silkily, and turned his attention to the waiter who had miraculously appeared at his side.

'No champagne for me; a soft drink, please,' Jules said coolly, not rising to the bait as he placed their order with the waiter in fluent Spanish. He really was a many-talented man but he was also a sarcastic swine; she didn't believe his compliment for a moment. She had no illusions about her looks. Attractive, yes, but 'exquisitely beautiful' was overdoing the hyperbole just a tad even to try and charm the dimmest female.

A wry smile twisted her mouth. Jules considered herself a reasonably intelligent adult woman, with a good career doing what she loved. In life as in business luck and timing was everything. Sadly for her mother, she had had no say in when her illness had struck. Jules could think *if only* it had been a year or two later, and at her worst moments *if only* it had been just six weeks sooner, then Jules would not have invested all their capital and the bank loan in the house and business. But her real wish was *if only* her wonderful mother had never taken ill at all.

Bad timing... Whatever, the reality was she needed money and she needed it now and, whether she liked it or not, Rand was her only hope. Unfortunately he held the purse strings. She knew the amount she needed would barely dent the value of her father's estate. But whether this autocratic man would give it to her, she was not so sure. Then any hope Jules had harboured that he might have forgotten about the past was dashed with his next words.

'So.' Rand returned his attention to her. 'I have ordered the seafood special; take my word, you will love it. I do.' He paused, and Jules felt her heart flutter in her breast, hypnotised by the smouldering warmth in his dark eyes. 'I love this place.' He leant back and waved an elegant hand in a gesture at the view and looked around. Released from the magnetic pull of his powerful gaze, Jules concentrated on steadying her breathing, but stifled a gasp of outrage as he continued. 'I must admit I was surprised you gave up the opportunity to live in this wonderful climate with a wealthy father and the prospect of a handsome husband for the doubtful pleasures of the British climate. Dare I assume you have changed your mind?' he prompted cynically.

He was doing it again, insulting her; did he take her for a fool or what? 'No, I have not. People are more important than places,' Jules said tightly.

'Forgive me for saying so, but that sounds rather strange coming from a girl like you.'

'You know nothing about me,' Jules shot back, bristling with anger at his implication.

'True.' Rand leant back in his chair as the waiter appeared with a jug of juice and two glasses, eyeing Jules though narrowed eyes. Amazingly she looked quite genuine in her indignation. He had to admit she was one hell of an actress, and he wondered what else she was good at. He could see the rise and fall of her firm breast beneath the soft linen of her jacket, and again felt a sudden tightening in his groin area he had some difficulty controlling.

Leaning forward to allow his body to subside, he filled a glass with juice. 'I am so embroiled in my work, I have trouble keeping track of the side issues.' Rand straightened and held out the glass of orange juice. 'But it is good to see you again.'

Jules felt the colour rise in her cheeks. 'Side issue' said it all, which was all she ever had been to her father or any other man. She reached out and took the glass from him, his long fingers accidentally brushing hers, and felt the tingling effect of his touch right up her arm. But as she controlled her shock her green eyes clashed with deep brown. Was it mockery she saw in the dark depths?

'Yes, well…' She cleared her throat, refusing to let her simmering anger show. 'Given you are so busy, perhaps we can combine lunch with business. I would hate to take up too much of your precious time,' she suggested, taking control of the situation and, lifting the glass to her mouth, she took a long, cooling swallow.

'As you like,' Rand said with a dismissive shrug of his broad shoulders. 'After all, I am here on behalf of your late father. Perhaps an enquiry on your part about his last illness would not go amiss,' he prompted sardonically.

'I had heard nothing from my father in seven years until you called to tell me he was ill. A heart attack, I believe you said, and I have no reason to disbelieve you,' she offered. 'For all I know he could have married again. I might even have a brother or sister I know nothing about,' she suggested dryly, 'but I am sure you can enlighten me.' Rand was not going to intimidate her and she boldly held his dark gaze, her own expression, she hoped, one of cool concern.

Her father and her ex-fiancé Enrique had been two of a kind. Arrogant, autocratic tyrants, who thought they could do what they wanted and everyone else had to do as they were told. Jules and her mum had both suffered at their manipulative hands, and she had to be mad to put herself in Rand's power, she had no doubt he was just the same, but what choice did she have?

First her mother had discovered her husband had a mistress right under her nose, and years later Jules had caught Enrique, Rand's supposed friend, with Maria, Rand's fiancée… No, she was not going there, or she might lose her temper completely and tell Rand the truth.

But then again he might already know all about Maria's unfaithfulness. Maybe that was why he had not married her. Whatever… Jules was not going to ask…

'I'm sure my father was well looked after to the end.'

'Oh, he was,' Rand assured her smoothly. 'And to ease your mind I can tell you he never married again.' He paused, his eyes narrowed intently on her delicate face. He would stake his fortune Jules knew damn fine she was the closest living relative of her late father, but he was prepared to play her along for now. 'And there are no other *children*,' he emphasised with an edge of cynicism in his tone. 'Though it pains me to admit, I had only seen Carlos half a dozen times in the last few years. I have a very efficient manager in the Santiago office and I don't come to Chile very often, but luckily I was staying at the ranch when he took ill. Too much red meat and too many cigars, a small heart attack that even the doctor thought was nothing too serious, and then a massive one and he died three days later. I attended the funeral, of course.'

'Good for you,' Jules said swiftly. 'I am glad he had someone with him.' Not that her father was ever alone, living on a ranch with several staff and never without a woman, as far as Jules knew. He had hardly needed Jules as well. But the constant mention of her father was churning up memories she preferred to forget and, pinning a smile on her face, she forced herself to look up into his eyes.

'But to be honest I did not really know him very well—a few weeks' holiday every summer for four years. You knew him much better than I.' She saw a brief flare of some powerful emotion on his face, but was quickly reassured when his firm lips parted into a reciprocal smile.

'You're right, of course; all the more reason why you must stay awhile,' Rand declared adamantly. 'Ah! The food has arrived. Let's enjoy our lunch.' He smiled again, his dark eyes mesmerising her. 'I have a very large appetite and it badly needs filling.' Jules blinked and tore her gaze away. Crude, she thought, and colour flooded her face at his suggestive comment, but she went pale as he added, 'We can talk about your father later when we get to the ranch.'

'The ranch?' she parroted, her eyes widening in puzzlement.

'Don't worry, I have made all the arrangements. After missing your father's funeral I knew you would want to visit his grave as soon as possible,' he said and she could only agree.

# CHAPTER THREE

JULES slid into the back seat of the car and briefly closed her eyes. Her father's grave... She sighed and opened her eyes, feeling guilty. It should have been her making the suggestion, not Rand Carducci. She had given him yet another black mark to hold against her. At the rate she was going she would be lucky if the man would even give her the time of day, let alone money.

Still she straightened in the seat as Rand slid in beside her; now was the ideal opportunity to state her case. Whatever her father had belatedly bequeathed her, could she convert it into money and how fast? That was basically what she wanted to know. If not she would just have to swallow her pride and ask outright for money. It was at least an hour's drive to the Diez property. With a bit of luck she could reach some agreement with Rand by the time they arrived at the hacienda. A quick visit to her father's grave and maybe even back to

England on the next plane tomorrow. There was no real reason for her to stay a week.

Feeling much more optimistic, Jules turned slightly and looked at him. He was smiling, a good omen, she thought, but before she could open her mouth he forestalled her.

'I hope you don't mind, Jules, but I have some work to catch up on.' His brief smile vanished as he lifted a leather briefcase onto his lap and flicked the lid open.

'Of course not.' Bang went her plan to get everything sorted before they arrived at the ranch. The great Rand Carducci had much more important business to attend to than her problem. On his list of priorities she obviously came very low in the pecking order. She supposed she should be honoured he had even deigned to spend the afternoon with her—but she didn't feel it. Instead she felt resentment simmering inside her.

'I can always reacquaint myself with the scenery, I suppose,' she said sarcastically. But her sarcasm was wasted on him.

'You do that.' And without so much as glancing at her, he lifted a sheaf of papers from the briefcase and, in moments, with an elegant gold pen in his hand, he was completely involved in his work.

Through the thick fringe of her eyelashes Jules studied him at her leisure, her eyes roaming over his profile, noting the typical frown, and down over his broad shoulders, slightly hunched as he studied the papers he was holding. Jules discovered that her gaze was riveted to his long-fingered, elegant hands, her pulse rate increasing as she stared at them. Gentle but exciting, she guessed, and abruptly she tore her eyes away and looked out of the window. Where on earth had the erotic thought come from? she wondered with a shiver.

Fixing her attention on the passing scenery, the land dry and parched with the heat of the summer, she was vividly reminded of the first time she had travelled this way. Then she had been bursting with enthusiasm and hope, longing to meet her father, and now eleven years later she was returning to visit his grave.

Tears pricked at the back of her eyes. He had loved this land with a passion, a commitment he had never been able to feel for anything or anyone else. Certainly not her, or her mother, Jules thought sadly; she could only pray it had been enough for him in the end.

As for her, unless her father had made some monetary provision for her in the codicil to his will so she could help her mother, she might very soon end up bankrupt or, worse, an orphan.

Her mother had recovered well from her operation and was working part-time, and looking forward to the treatment that they both hoped would seal her recovery. But she had not been happy at Jules coming here. Her mother thought it seemed mercenary, and that they did not need anything from the man as they had done very well on their own. It was only when Jules had said it was probably only an ornament or the like that she had been left, but the all-expenses-paid holiday was worth having and she could do with a break before her mother started her treatment, that Liz had agreed. Liz had no idea of Jules' cash-flow problem, and Jules had no intention of telling her.

Stifling a sigh, she turned a narrow-eyed glance on Rand. It was all in the hands of this one man, and she was beginning to get the distinct impression he was deliberately avoiding discussing her father's estate. Three hours later Jules was convinced of it...

They had arrived at the Diez ranch mid-afternoon. Sanchez, the estate manager, had been at the hacienda to meet them. Rand had been greeted with a hug, and Jules had rather tentatively held out her hand. She had been worried how her absence from the funeral would look to a man who had spent decades working for her father.

But she need not have worried as Sanchez ignored her hand and gave her a big hug as well; that did much to relieve her anxiety in returning to the ranch. Sanchez was the man who had taught her to ride a horse, and she had spent many a happy hour roaming over the ranch with him in the past.

Sanchez's wife, Donna, the housekeeper, was equally welcoming, and to Jules' amazement Donna was very obviously pregnant. She congratulated her and was rewarded with a smile and a hug. To Jules' knowledge Donna had to be at least forty and had been trying to have a baby as long as Jules could remember.

Ten minutes later, seated in the salon, a glass of champagne in her hand Rand had insisted she drink in a toast to her return, Jules glanced around her, the memories rushing back.

She had been so impressed by the house as a teenager, but she was nowhere near as impressed now. The building, the furniture and fittings were beautiful, and immaculately cared for exactly as she remembered, but with maturity she realised the house lacked any sense of home. A portrait in oil by a famous Dutch artist dominated the hall, but there were no personal photographs, and nothing to say who had lived here.

'So, Jules, how does it feel to be back, dare I say, home?'

The voice was cool, the words faintly mocking. She glanced up at Rand standing in front of the elegantly carved fireplace, one hand idly twisting the champagne flute between his long fingers, the expression in his black eyes impossible to read.

Out of nowhere came the conviction that this was a man who would dare anything to get what he wanted. He was poised like some mighty eagle, his physical strength evident beneath the impeccably tailored pale grey suit, waiting to rip her to shreds given the chance.

Jules chose her words with care. 'The house has not changed at all. But it is not, nor ever will be, my home; that is not why I am here,' she said calmly, and was astonished how normal her voice sounded.

'No, of course, you are here to visit your father's grave.' There was a gleam of mocking amusement in his black eyes, and Jules felt a sudden surge of pure anger. Damn him, he had been playing around with her all afternoon, and she was sick of it. Slamming her glass down on the table, she leapt to her feet.

'Look, Rand,' she began, walking towards him, ordering herself to control her anger, instinct telling her she could not afford to lose her temper with him. She managed to resist the temptation by curling her hands into fists at her sides as she stopped in front of him.

'You might have all the time in the world for visiting. Whatever, but I don't.' Her cool expression did not betray a thing but her mind was working frantically. 'I have a very busy work schedule and I want to get back to

England as soon as possible, so can we get down to business now?' She looked at him with candid green eyes, trying to see him as a business acquaintance, nothing more. For some reason her body sensed its weakness next to his, and she didn't like the feeling. She wanted to get away from his disturbing presence and fast. 'What exactly did my father leave me, and is it negotiable?' And she hoped like hell it was more than the ornament she had suggested to her mother.

A flicker of anger showed briefly in his eyes. 'I know a bakery is essential for any town, but it is hardly rocket science. I'm sure your staff are perfectly capable of running the business without you. You know what they say—all work and no pleasure…' Cupping her chin with one strong hand, he tilted her face up, one long finger gently caressing her cheek. 'There is no need to rush, Jules,' he drawled softly. 'We have a lot to catch up on, or is that what you are afraid of?'

His derogatory comment about her small business left her speechless, and it did not help that her nerve endings tingled at the contact of flesh on flesh. So she wasn't in his league business-wise, but then very few in the world were, and she wasn't about to justify her chosen career to him.

As far as she was concerned they had nothing to catch up on. They had barely been friends, unless he meant Enrique and Maria, she thought, horrified. Surely he didn't want a blow-by-blow account? Her green eyes, stormy, collided with deep, dark brown. 'Not you, that's for sure,' she snapped. But then his smallest finger trailed over her full lips, and a shiver lanced through her slender body and she knew she had lied. Because suddenly she was desperately afraid, afraid of what Rand was making her feel.

'Well, if you're sure about that, then you won't mind this,' he declared huskily.

She could feel her heart racing, the blood rushing through her veins. Involuntarily she swayed towards him, drowning in the darkening depths of his eyes, unaware that her own registered her sensual shock. The hand on her cheek slid to clasp the back of her head as his other hand snaked around her waist and up her spine and she was pulled against the solid wall of his chest.

Her stomach appeared to perform a somersault as she felt the strength of his thighs pressed against her and she trembled in a mixture of fear and excitement. She did not know what was happening to her. The fear kept her still in his embrace and she looked up with wide, confused eyes as his dark head lowered to hers.

His lips closed over hers, moving gently, persuasively, and Jules felt something melting inside her. His hand twisted the braid of her hair around his wrist and held her face up to his as he whispered softly against her mouth, 'I have been wanting to do that since the moment I set eyes on you today, and if you're honest so have you.'

'No.' She opened her mouth to deny him with the tiny atom of common sense she had left, and in that instant his firm lips captured hers again. Taking the opportunity she had inadvertently offered, his tongue intruded with a shattering sensuality, exploring the moist dark interior of her mouth with a no longer gentle but a hungry, demanding passion. The hand at her back pressed her closer to his hard length, one long leg nudging between her thighs.

It was electrifying, and so unexpected. For the first time in her life Jules felt the searing heat of physical arousal. The few kisses she had exchanged with Enrique in the past had never made her feel this way. Every pulse in her body went haywire and she had an incredible urge to press herself closer to the rock-solid strength of Rand's great body. Her mouth came alive beneath the pressure of his, and she returned his kiss with a helpless, hungry urgency, her arms sliding involuntarily around his neck.

The kiss went on and on, Rand claiming her mouth with a fierce, possessive need and Jules felt a totally unfamiliar tide of emotion sweeping through her that she had no control over. Her rational mind shut down and she returned his ardour with greed, a fiery if less than expert desire she had not known she was capable of. She inhaled his heady scent and as his hand cupped one firm breast she felt the sudden painful tightening of her nipples. Finally she knew what it was to really want a man sexually, the primitive hunger tightening her belly, demanding some release from the fierce tension, the heat consuming her.

She heard Rand's low groan as he finally broke the kiss. Jules looked up at him, dazed and breathless, as he gently removed her arms from around his neck and held them at her sides. She was still leaning against him, because she doubted her legs would fully support her.

Rand stared down into her hazy green eyes, his own a cloudy black. He reached out and brushed a stray curl from her flushed cheek.

'Skinny little Jules,' he drawled softly. 'Who would have thought you would develop into such a sexy lady? And that beneath that beautiful pale exterior lurked so much passion.' And he eased her away from him.

Jules blinked, her mind beginning to clear. 'No,' she denied, and felt a shaming surge of colour sweep up her face, mortified by her own response. 'You caught me unawares.'

Rand's hooded lids dropped over his black eyes, masking his expression, and for a long moment he studied the scarlet-faced beautiful girl before him. *You and I both,* he almost confessed, shocked rigid in more ways than one by the powerful rush of desire and the overwhelming need to possess her... It was years, if ever, since a woman had turned him on so hard, so fast and so achingly… For a man who took pride in his ability to control everything and everyone, he wasn't sure he liked the feeling.

Finally taking a deep breath and with a shrug of his broad shoulders, he said, 'If you say so.' And, avoiding looking at the bewitching Jules, he pushed back his sleeve and glanced at the fine platinum watch on his wrist. 'If you will excuse me for a while, I have some business to discuss with Sanchez. Donna will show you to your room, and you can get changed.' It wasn't in his nature to run away, but in this instant he had to, or he was in real danger of taking Jules where she stood, and losing himself in the incredible splendour of her lush body.

'Changed.' Jules, in her confused state of mind, only managed to focus properly on his last word. 'I can't—I have no clothes.' They were all at the hotel in Santiago.

A naked Jules… That was an image he could do without right at the moment. But even so he couldn't help himself. His gaze roamed with heated masculine appreciation down the length of her body to her feet. Noting the high-heeled sandals that accentuated the long shapeliness of her legs, then travelling upwards again in a slow, lingering appraisal of the smooth curve of her hips, and the upper swell of her high proud breasts, revealed by the lapels of her jacket.

'A little larger in the breast, I think…no?' He lifted one black brow in mocking query.

If that was a question Jules had no intention of answering, and, red with embarrassment, she stared mutely at him.

'But as for the rest,' Rand continued quickly,' you are still the long-limbed girl I remember. I think you will find the trousers you left behind will fit. I'll collect you in about an hour. Sanchez will saddle up the horses and we can take a ride to your father's grave, before the light goes.'

Jules opened her mouth to object, but Rand was already exiting the room, the click of the door as he shut it behind him finally registering in her churning mind that she was alone.

She was still staring at the closed door a long moment later. What had happened? Where was her cool reserve? Her businesslike attitude? Taking a few slow, deep breaths, she felt marginally better. So Rand had kissed her! So what? She was not a complete novice, she had been kissed before, she told herself sternly. But never like that and never with such devastating results, a tiny devilish voice prompted in her head... But more importantly, she realised as she made her way upstairs, Rand had expertly deflected her from pursuing the subject of her inheritance yet again...

'I was right, a perfect fit,' Rand opined as she walked down the stairs slightly less than an hour later.

'Clever you,' Jules snapped, her temper fraying at the edges. It had been a shock to discover, on being shown to her old room, that the few clothes she had left behind at eighteen, mainly trousers and tops, were all cleaned and pressed and hanging in the wardrobe. There wasn't much as her mother had been going to bring her carefully chosen trousseau with her when she arrived the day before the wedding. Jules had naturally assumed her father would have got rid of everything belonging to her so it was a terrible shock to see the wedding dress still in Cellophane hanging in the closet. That he had kept everything somehow saddened her; perhaps he had cared for her in his own way...

After a quick shower, she had dressed in a pair of well-washed jeans, and teamed them with a white knit cotton shirt, and to her amazement even her old riding boots had been cleaned and polished.

It didn't help her temper that Rand had been right, and seeing him lounging against the door waiting for her simply made her feel worse.

As she reached the bottom of the stairs her eyes skimmed over his tall, impressive figure. Her heart skipped a beat, and it took all her self-control to walk towards him. Gone was the business suit, and in its place the three top buttons of his black checked shirt were undone, revealing a glimpse of tanned chest and dark curling hair. Black denim jeans clung to his long legs like a second skin, and the hair on the back of her neck began to prickle as she walked forward.

He looked dark and somehow dangerous. Perhaps it was his very stillness or the cool arrogance of his expression as he waited for *her* to approach *him* that gave her the weird notion he resembled a large, sleek panther. A predator that had stalked her all day and he was now ready to pounce.

With a brief shake of her head she stopped in front of him and glanced up into his hard face. 'Let's go, my time is limited and I do want to get back to Santiago tonight,' she said firmly, and strolled on past him through the open front door and into the courtyard.

'I am at your command.' His husky chuckle followed her out into the brilliant light of the afternoon sun.

Jules blinked, and then gasped, and ran across to where Sanchez stood holding the bridles of two horses. 'You still have her.' She sent a beaming smile Sanchez's way, her green eyes sparkling. 'Polly, my pony.' She rubbed the neck of the small piebald mare with a gentle hand and pressed her lips to the silky coat. 'I can't believe she is still here.'

Sanchez's sombre face broke into a broad grin.' Your father insisted we kept her in peak condition—' he spoke in Spanish '—just in case you returned.'

Jules blinked back tears, and nodded. 'Thank you, Sanchez.'

Rand watched the little scene played out and, with a cynical smile twisting his firm mouth, he took the bridle of his horse, a large black stallion, and swung himself into the saddle. Jules showed more emotion over a horse than she did over her own father.

'I thought you were in a hurry, Jules,' he prompted curtly, watching her cuddling the pony's neck, and for a second he remembered the feel of those same slender arms around his own and shifted uncomfortably in the saddle. 'Mount up,' he commanded gruffly.

Jules did as she was told, and, gripping the reins in one hand, she took the small posy of flowers Sanchez held up for her with the other.

'For your father.'

Carlos Diez had been laid to rest in a small private burial plot situated in the lee of a small hill to protect against the elements. Jules stood over his grave while Rand held the horses off to one side, in the shade of a solitary old pine tree.

Jules stared down at the polished marble headstone. It saddened her to think of her father dying alone without family, and the tears formed in her eyes and slid silently down her pale cheeks. Jules had never really known her father, not the inner man, what made him function, his hopes and fears. All she had seen in the few short months she had actually spent with him was a handsome old man, who had kindly given her Polly and encouraged her to learn to ride.

A man who had given her the freedom of the ranch, and taken great pleasure in introducing her to his neighbours. A man proud of his land and his accomplishments on the polo field. And for a while proud of his daughter, he had rejoiced in her engagement to his neighbour's son, and happily arranged the wedding.

But he had also been a man who had never allowed Jules to travel outside the boundaries of their immediate neighbours. Who had never let her see the side of his life he'd spent in Santiago two or three days a week. She had heard the rumours of his lady friends, but had thought nothing of it, too involved in exploiting the delights of what for her was a foreign country and her teenage love affair. It was only when she had returned to England broken-hearted that her mother had told her the true facts about her marriage, and Jules had realised the rumours had probably all been true, and the extent of her father's manipulations.

Tears blinding her eyes, she accepted the finality of his death, and yet she wished with all her heart she had had one last chance to talk to him. But life was all about choices and she had made hers when she had stayed with her sick mother.

Jules dropped to her knees and placed the posy of flowers on the mound of earth. 'You understand now, Papa, forgive me,' she murmured, and silently mouthed a prayer for her dear father and made the sign of the cross. Rising slowly to her feet, she glanced sightlessly around, her mind full of memories of the past.

Damn it! She was crying. Rand took a step towards her. He disliked weeping women, or, more to the point, he did not know how to deal with them. His dark eyes narrowed intently on Jules' small pale face, and he stilled. In his experience the few occasions a lady friend had subjected him to a crying jag, usually when he'd been saying goodbye, it had not been a pretty sight; red face and blotchy skin were usually the result. But he might have guessed Jules cried beautifully, the teardrops running over her smooth cheeks like pearls gleaming in the sun, and as he watched she lifted her hands to her face and brushed them away.

Totally oblivious to Rand's scrutiny, Jules took a deep unsteady breath and focused on the other graves in the plot where her father was buried. There were only two more. The first Carlos Diez and his wife, born well over a hundred years ago, their only son and his wife, and now Jules' father.

Her gaze was drawn back to the newest addition, and she felt tears burn her eyes once more as she stared at the single name engraved in gold in the cold marble. Her father...Carlos Diez the third...and, with his sister Ester an exile in Italy...the last...

Not much of a dynasty, she thought sadly. The first Carlos Diez must have dreamt of much more when he'd first bought this land. And in that moment Jules could almost understand her father's behaviour towards her, and forgive him. If she had married Enrique and the ranches had joined, someone with Diez blood would still have lived on the land.

A deep sigh of sadness and regret escaped her, and, lifting her head, she looked beyond the burial plot and wondered what the future held for the land now.

Rand, sensing she was ready to leave, led the horses towards her. Suddenly aware of his presence, Jules straightened her shoulders and looked up into his ruggedly attractive face.

'It's the end of an era, so what is going to happen to the ranch now?' she asked curiously.

He shrugged his broad shoulders. 'It's debatable, but discussing the division of the property over your father's grave is hardly appropriate even for you. The questions can wait until we get back to the house.' His two hands closed roughly around her narrow waist and lifted her clear off her feet and onto Polly's back. 'You owe your father that much respect, at the very least,' Rand drawled sardonically.

Jules flushed at his insulting comment, and quickly averted her eyes. He thought she was worried about her father's legacy, but it hadn't been that at all; it was simply that her last thought before he'd spoken had been about the land. But she was feeling too fragile to put him straight, so she ignored him and urged her horse forward instead.

Rand followed behind on his black stallion, his dark eyes skimming over the stiff set of her slender shoulders and her rigid spine. If she didn't relax she would fall off the damn pony, and it would be his fault. He couldn't help his cynical nature, but even he knew he had over-stepped the bounds of decency with his last crack.

Reining up alongside her, he glanced at her. 'Jules, I'm sorry. I know you are upset.' He broke eye contact for a moment as the stallion moved restlessly beneath him, eager to go.

Jules noted the muscles in his strong thighs flex as he controlled the big animal. 'I'm fine,' she murmured, her mouth suddenly dry, and her fingers tightened convulsively on Polly's reins. Or she would be, she told herself, once she was away from Rand, the ranch, this country for good.

It was odd but at home in England she was a cool, calm, level-headed woman. She never had any trouble with erotic thoughts about men. Yet the moment she set foot in Chile it was as if the Latin half of her genes were suddenly switched on. The first time she had taken one look at Enrique and imagined herself in love. Now it was happening again with the totally unsuitable Rand Carducci. The only difference was with maturity she recognised it was not love, but lust.

'You're not fine and, unless you want to join your father prematurely, relax—you have nothing to worry about.'

Rand could be hinting that she stood to gain something from her father's estate, she supposed, but as for his choice of words nothing 'to worry about', he didn't know the half. Jules sighed, and made a deliberate effort to relax tight muscles before glancing across at him. Man and beast blurred into one, a dark, dangerous entity that sent a shiver of fear skidding down her spine.

'Right at this moment I don't think I care,' Jules finally responded quietly, reluctantly admitting Rand was too powerful, too compellingly masculine for her to cope with right now. The reality of her father's death, the ill health of her mother, the business, and the disturbing emotions Rand made her feel suddenly all combined to drain every drop of energy she had left.

'You're tired, you have had a long day, and probably a little jet lag,' Rand said as they approached the house, where Sanchez was waiting in the yard. Bringing his horse to a stop, Rand swiftly dismounted. 'Take care of the horses, please, Sanchez.' Reaching up, he grabbed Jules by the waist and swung her out of the saddle and to the ground. 'While I take care of Miss Julia—she is exhausted.'

'No, I am not.' Jules tried to protest, but, with Rand's large hands spanning her waist and held close to his hard, lean body, she did feel slightly peculiar. She could see the steady rise and fall of his great chest, and her nostrils filled with the seductive scent of man, horse and leather, and she stumbled against him. Rand held her closer.

'A long time since you have ridden, hmm?' His dark eyes, gleaming with what looked suspiciously like compassion, captured hers. 'Here, let me help you.' Curving one arm around her waist, he led her unresistingly into the cool interior of the house.

His arm fell from her waist and for a moment Jules felt deprived, but only a moment as, glancing around the familiar hall, she was vividly reminded of her purpose for being here, and determination stiffened her spine.

'A rest for you, I think.' Rand gestured to the stairs. Her time clock must be all to hell, what with the time difference between here and England.

'No,' Jules said curtly, and walked past him towards the study door, then stopped and turned. 'I came to Chile because according to you my father had added a codicil to his will leaving me something. You have been deliberately avoiding the issue all day; it is way past time we got down to business.'

# CHAPTER FOUR

His consideration was wasted on her, Rand thought cynically. Jules was as hard as stone. Strolling over to her, he reached around her waist, saw her flinch, and with a knowing smile opened the study door. 'After you, Jules,' he drawled, and watched her scuttle in before following and closing the door behind them.

Jules stopped in the centre of the room, slightly ashamed at her helpless reaction to Rand's close proximity and her hasty entrance. She glanced around and for a bone-chilling moment the memory of the last time she had been in this room with her father filled her mind. Eighteen, shocked, shattered and hurting, she had listened to her father declare she must do as he said or never darken his door again.

She shrugged her slender shoulders; memories could not hurt her now, and, turning, she stiffened.

Rand lazed back in the leather-winged chair behind her father's desk, looking as though he owned the place, and his stepmother Ester probably did, Jules thought. But, keeping her composure, she strolled over to a chair at the opposite side of the desk and sat down.

'I wondered how long you could control your impatience,' Rand opined, slanting her a mocking glance before consulting the watch on his tanned wrist. 'I make it almost six hours. Not bad, Jules.'

'Glad you approve—' she met his gaze without flinching '—but now can we stop the games and get down to the reason why I am here?'

'Certainly.' He picked up an official-looking document. 'Your father's will, dated seven years ago; he was angry with you at the time.' He flicked it over the desk towards her. 'Read it and you will see you are not mentioned in it at all—basically there are a few bequests to staff and friends, the painting in the hall to me, and the rest goes to Ester.'

Jules picked it up, saw the date and heading and dropped it back on the table. 'I believe you, but can you be an executor and benefit from a will?' she asked with a frown. Not that she begrudged him the painting. Personally she thought it was awful, a portrait of a stern-faced man; her lips twitched—though quite appropriate for Rand.

'Executor, yes, a witness to a will, no,' Rand informed her shortly. 'But this is what concerns you.' He flicked a single sheet of paper across to her. 'He added a codicil duly witnessed and signed by the doctor and his nurse here in this room, a few days before he had the massive heart attack that killed him.'

She leant forward and picked up the document with a hand that shook. If it needed witnesses then at least her father had left her something tangible, and she immediately felt guilty for feeling relieved.

'Go ahead, read it; I can assure you it is genuine. I was with your father at the time.'

She took a deep steadying breath and began to read. It was blunt and to the point. Basically it stated if within six months of his demise his estranged daughter, Julia Diez, returned to Chile of her own free will and agreed to marry Randolfo Carducci and live in Chile for one year she would inherit a half-share in the ranch with her aunt Ester. If the said Julia Diez did not comply with the conditions as set out within the allotted time the codicil was null and void, and his estate passed as stated in the body of his will to Ester Carducci.

Jules' mouth hung open in shocked amazement, and her green eyes widened in dawning horror as she read her father's signature, her brain registering there was no affection in a single word. Her father had never cared for her at all; he was still trying to manipulate her from the grave. How awful was that?

What little colour she had leeched from her face. She couldn't believe what she had read, and read it again. Slowly she lifted her head, and looked across the desk to where Rand was sitting, his dark face expressionless, watching her.

'You know what is in this?' she finally asked.

'Yes, of course, I was there when he wrote it.'

'And you let him,' she said with a negative shake of her head. 'You're as crazy as he was.'

'No, I simply pandered to the wishes of a lonely old man at the time.'

'But according to this I have to marry you and live here for a year to inherit anything.' Her voice rose incredulously as the sheer arrogance of her father's request finally hit her.

'Would it be such a hardship?' Rand drawled softly, the question faintly mocking.

Carlos had written the codicil after his first small heart attack. At the time Rand had agreed simply because he had thought if it kept Carlos happy, then why argue? Plus the doctor had assured him Carlos could live for years if he was careful, and Rand had judged with his intervention father and daughter would be reconciled, and a new will drawn up long before anything happened to the old man. Rand had called Jules in the first step to effecting reconciliation between father and daughter the same day.

A few more calls to Jules and the sudden death of Carlos and Rand was forced to admit he had been wrong... As for Jules—originally thinking she deserved some consideration from her father, Rand had changed his mind after speaking to her. She was obviously a heartless bitch and did not deserve a cent.

For a long moment Jules simply stared at Rand, her flesh prickling in sensual awareness, her green eyes helplessly studying his strikingly attractive face, and she almost said *no*. Shocked at where her thoughts were leading, Jules said hastily, 'I can't possibly marry you, and I certainly could not stop here for a year. I have commitments at home in England.'

Rand gave a short sharp laugh as the irony of the situation hit him. He had never had any intention of marrying her, and had been wondering how to get out of it with his honour intact and at the least possible expense, but it was still galling that Jules had beaten him to it with her refusal. 'A boyfriend, perhaps?' he asked.

'No, of course not.' In her agitation she told the truth without thought. 'But there is my mother, and I have a business to run, and friends. It is impossible.'

'Nothing is impossible—' he got to his feet and walked slowly around the desk and sat lightly on the edge in front of her '—if you try.'

He was much too close for comfort and Jules moved her legs slightly to avoid contact with his and stiffened in her seat. 'To you, maybe not—' her chin lifted '—but to we lesser mortals, quite frequently,' she said with feeling and looked directly up into his hard face. She caught the gleam of mocking amusement in his eyes and leapt to her feet on a sudden surge of anger. Damn him, he was doing it again. He thought the whole situation was funny. 'It might be funny to you, but not to me,' she cried.

'Steady.' Rand caught her wrists and held her in front of him. He had to rethink quickly. Jules wanted something, and it would be interesting to see how far she would go to get it. 'Don't take everything so seriously. I know your father's demand is ridiculous in this day and age,' he opined in a conciliatory tone. 'I am no more looking for a wife than you are a husband.'

His hands on her wrists made her flesh burn, and she remembered the heat of his kiss and for a moment she felt an odd flutter of what felt like disappointment in her heart. What was she thinking of? She didn't want to marry the man, she told herself furiously, hanging onto her anger. She glanced up at him and he was watching her with that dark intent gaze, and it made Jules nervous.

'What I can't understand is why you agreed in the first place?' she prompted with a shake of her head. 'There is nothing in it for you.' Some basic instinct told her she must tread warily around Rand if she wanted to salvage anything from this mess and help her mother.

'Would you believe altruism on my part? I wanted to keep Carlos happy, and because I mistakenly thought he would live for years and I also thought, arrogantly I admit, one call from me and you and Carlos would be reconciled, and the necessity for marriage negated.'

'Oh.' He was arrogant enough to think that, Jules had no doubt, and he had called her. 'So what do we do now?'

'Nothing you need worry about. I am great at finding a way around things,' he declared with the selfsame arrogance that ignited Jules' temper all over again.

'Nothing to worry about…and that is supposed to make me feel better. Ester gets the lot and I am left with nothing, but feeling better,' Jules mocked as the full import of the document sank in. 'Great for you, but not so hot for me.'

A flicker of anger showed briefly in his eyes. 'No, Jules—' he pulled her towards him '—that is not necessarily so. I am the sole executor and I can use my discretion,' he drawled softly, seductively. 'I am sure we can come to some amicable arrangement that will suit us both.'

Her wide eyes clashed with his, a gleam of hope in their emerald depths. 'How?'

'Well, for a start—' Rand straightened up and, dropping her wrists, lifted his hands to her shoulders '—you and I can try to become at the very least friends.' His gaze moved over her lovely face. 'We owe it to your father to try, if only for the one week you are scheduled to stay in Chile.'

A week… That was a hell of a lot better than a year, and with the shock clearing from her mind Jules began to think straight. 'My father must have known it was a ridiculous idea from the start, because a seriously wealthy man like you with a huge international business to control certainly could not have spent a year stuck on the ranch, never mind me.'

A deep husky chuckle greeted her remark. 'Your father was as stubborn as an ox and a chauvinist of the first order. I doubt if my convenience even entered his head.'

'Flaming typical,' Jules snorted.

'Yes, well, never mind that now.' Slipping an arm around her shoulder, he urged her across to the black hide sofa. 'Sit down. I'll get Donna to serve coffee and we can discuss what we are going to do.'

Ten minutes later Jules drained the dregs of her coffee the housekeeper had provided, placed the cup on the table and, perching on the edge of the sofa, she turned her head slightly and looked at Rand sprawled beside her, his long legs stretched out before him in casual ease. He looked as if he hadn't a care in the world. But then he probably hadn't—it was Jules who was desperate for money from her father's estate.

'So what do you suggest?' she demanded impatiently. Sitting close to Rand was playing havoc with her nerves.

'What exactly do you want?' Rand demanded. His gaze dipped to her lips then lifted to meet her eyes, his own flat and hard, his face suddenly deadly serious. 'That is the question, but before you answer allow me to give you some facts. The ranch on paper is worth maybe a million in pound sterling, not a fortune by any means. Plus in reality the place just about makes enough to cover the overheads and the employees' wages. It is a way of life rather than a money-spinner. Basically because it isn't really a big enough unit in today's ranching terms.'

Rand stood up and turned to look down at where she sat. 'It is up to you, Jules,' he said softly, his dark eyes narrowed intently on her face. 'If you want to stay here for a year I will marry you.' Where the hell had that come from? A muscle pulsed in his jaw; it was not what he had intended to say at all.

Startled at his 'I will marry you', Jules glanced up over his great body and felt hot colour surge in her cheeks as for a heady moment she imagined being married to Rand. Until he pointed out he had no choice.

'I can hardly refuse without being called a rogue or worse as Ester would inherit everything if I did.' Rand's eyes narrowed, probing her delicate face. He could see she was tempted, and—damn it!—even knowing what kind of person she was, so was he, and swiftly he continued. 'But I think between us we can reach a much simpler monetary solution.'

Jules felt a peculiar chill as she listened to his words, a sense of having suddenly lost all control of the situation almost overwhelming her. Rand was a shrewd businessman, a sharp operator, and she knew she needed all her wits about her to deal with him. Composing her features into what she hoped was a polite mask, she had to swallow hard before she could speak.

'I don't want the ranch, I don't want to stay here,' she said in a firm, soft voice. But she couldn't lie and add the obvious, I don't want you, because looking at Rand all dark and brooding she knew she did, at least on a sexual level. 'But...' it was an admission she hated having to make, but it had to be made '...I do want some money.'

Rand's face hardened. It was no more than he'd expected, but it was strangely disappointing to hear Jules voice it out loud. 'How much?' he said harshly. 'Let me guess—half the value,' he drawled sardonically.

'No,' Jules denied immediately. 'Nothing like that. I thought—' and she mentioned the sum that would cover the cost of her mother's treatment for the three years.

'Per annum, I take it,' he prompted. It was not a lot of money, and in all honour, as he had never intended fulfilling his part of the codicil and marrying his inherited bride, she was entitled to something. But if she thought she was going to get that much a month she was in for a rude awakening. 'Or per month?' he said cynically.

'Good God, no. I meant a one-off payment, and then you will never hear from me again,' Jules declared adamantly. 'I promise.'

'You are joking.' Rand's eyes flared incredulously. 'You can't be serious.' It was no great amount. He spent much more than that on his cars in a year. So what game was she playing?

'Well, maybe a third less,' Jules offered, quickly adjusting the figure. In two years' time, providing the catering business flourished, her cash-flow problems would be sorted and the cost of her mother's treatment would not be a problem. Tilting back her head, she looked up at him and waited.

'A third less.' His strong face hard and taut, his eyes, as cold as ice, clashed with hers almost accusingly. 'You don't mean that.'

'Or even half,' Jules offered, panicking, She would settle for enough to get her mother's treatment for one year if she had to. It would give her the breathing space she needed to make up the rest. 'But I need it immediately.'

There was a short silence.

'No,' Rand remarked in a strained voice. The beautiful green eyes that held his were wide and pleading and there was no doubt she was deadly serious. For once in his life he was speechless. If she was a gold-digger, she was the strangest one he had ever met. He watched as the light of hope left her eyes and her slender shoulders slumped, and he realised she thought he had refused to give her even that piffling amount.

'No, Jules, I mean I think we can come to some arrangement with the first figure you mentioned,' he added abruptly and he wondered how on earth she and her mother ran a small successful business, if they were so unworldly about money. Still, it wasn't his problem.

He had made a disturbing discovery when going through the family papers after Carlos' death, and he just wanted the estate settled quickly to the satisfaction of all parties, and with a reasonably clear conscience, so he could get back to his own life and work. He had already set the wheels in motion to do just that and he did not want Jules throwing a spanner in the works.

Jules felt an overwhelming tide of relief flood through her. 'You're sure?' His black eyes glittered with humour or irritation, she wasn't sure which as he reached down, grasped her hand and pulled her to her feet.

'Positive.' He chuckled softly. 'I will write the cheque out for you now. But I do have to make a few conditions. First, you stay here the week rather than the hotel as a token gesture to your father's request you live here. You owe him that much. Plus it will take me that long to get everything finalised.'

'But my clothes, my luggage.'

'Not to worry, I will send the driver to collect your luggage in the morning.'

'Okay. Yes,' she agreed tentatively, and felt an odd little leap of her pulse as he smiled crookedly down into her eyes. 'And...?' she prompted.

'Second, if in the next few days you change your mind and want to stay, I will enter into a marriage of convenience with you on the strict understanding we divorce at the end of the year, and if you then want to sell your half of the property you must sell it to me.'

Trying to ignore the sensations his hand on her arm and the nearness of his great body aroused in her, she grinned slightly. 'That certainly won't happen.'

'Good, though it does not do much for my ego.' A faintly mocking smile creased his hard face. 'But I will draw up the option-to-sell paper and get you to sign it just in case you change your mind.' If she agreed he could get the business end tied up straight away, which was what her father should have done in the first place, Rand realised grimly, given the family situation. But he let nothing of his thoughts show on his face as he added, 'And finally I will personally escort you to the airport at the end of the week and see you safely on a flight back to England.' He let go of her hand and stepped back a pace, folding his arms across his broad chest, and stared at her, considering. 'With one more proviso—I have to answer to Ester when I return to Italy, so...'

'But surely she will be delighted knowing she is keeping her childhood home?' Jules cut in questioningly, a puzzled frown marking her smooth brow.

'She is not bothered, she hasn't been here in forty years, but she is bothered that she has never met her brother's only child. I have strict instructions to reiterate the open invitation she gave you some years ago to visit her in Italy.'

'I don't know...'

'If you can spare the time from your obviously very busy schedule,' Rand prompted sardonically.

He had agreed to give her the money she needed, but his dig left her in no doubt he still thought she was lower than a snake for not turning up when her father had been dying. Well, she was not about to explain herself again. 'I'll try.'

'Make sure you do.'

She sent him a dubious glance. His arms were no longer folded over his broad chest and he had moved slightly closer, and something in his face made her pause. 'Do you want me to?' she asked uncertainly.

A strong hand reached out and engulfed one of hers. 'Oh, yes.' He nodded, his sensuous mouth twisting in a wry smile. 'I want you to, Jules.'

The warmth of his hand was somehow re-assuring. 'Personally I would quite like to get to know Aunt Ester...' She smiled softly. 'My only aunty, as it happens.' The summer Ester had found out Jules existed from Rand, she had written to Jules expressing a wish to meet her and her mother if they ever visited Italy. Her mother had said it was up to Jules if she wanted to write back, but she had no desire to get mixed up with the Diez family ever again. Jules was no letter-writer and had sent a Christmas card thanking Ester for the offer, and they had exchanged Christmas cards ever since but that was it.

'Then we are agreed?' Rand asked huskily. 'About everything.' And squeezed her hand. Maybe she was not quite the heartless, money-hungry woman he had her down for after all.

'Yes, agreed,' she murmured.

There was a long silence as they stared at each other, the tension stretching between them an almost tangible thing. The tension of two people, with a fierce physical attraction between them, that neither one wanted to admit to. At the same time they had committed to spending the week together, and staying as friends in the future.

Jules wondered what she had let herself in for, and her eyes widened as his hand slowly inched up her bare arm, giving her ample opportunity to move away if she wanted to, but she didn't. Her pale skin burned beneath his touch and as his hand slid around her shoulder to gently cup the back of her head her slender body quivered with sensual awareness.

Rand felt her reaction, and suddenly the next few days looked very promising. Eventually he would walk away from Jules the same way she had walked away from Enrique and her father without a thought of the consequences. But in the meantime...

'Shall we seal the deal with a kiss?' His voice was low and incredibly seductive.

Humour gleamed in the eyes that held hers, and Jules couldn't answer him, her breath trapped in her throat as his head lowered and he kissed her.

She raised her hands to his chest in token resistance, but his mouth was firm and sure and she instantly surrendered. Desire shot through her body like a lightning bolt and she realised she had been aching for this since their first kiss a few short hours ago. She felt the touch of his tongue and her lips parted and the kiss deepened. Her hands slid up over his chest to wind around his neck and she melted against him.

How long the kiss lasted Jules didn't know, but when he eventually lifted his mouth from hers she felt dazed and her legs were threatening to give way beneath her. It was only due to the fact Rand's arm was wrapped around her waist holding her tight against his strong body that she didn't crumble to the floor in a heap.

'Thank God we are not real cousins,' Rand murmured, a grin twisting his sensuous lips. 'Or we could be in real trouble.'

Jules gazed at him with bedazzled eyes. 'Trouble?' Once again only focusing on his last word.

'You know what I mean.' His hand moved from her head to smooth some stray tendrils of hair back from her face, and lingered on her cheek. 'The physical attraction between us is electric, has been from the moment we met today.'

'Uh-huh,' Jules said. There was little point in denying it, plastered to his body.

'And we have the time to explore all the possibilities,' he husked, his long fingers tracing the line of her jaw, the swollen contours of her lips. *Dio!* But she was beautiful. Rand uttered a silent curse. He was supposed to be closing a deal with her. So why the hell was he staring into her incredible green eyes, like a halfwit, with a certain part of his anatomy so hard he was hurting? Abruptly his arms fell to his sides. 'But first we must get business out of the way. I'll get my briefcase and write the cheque out now.'

Jules sat on the edge of the bed, in the room she had stayed in as a teenager, and stared at the cheque in her hand. She read the name of the bank and the figures over again, and then her gaze was drawn to the bold black signature in the corner. When Rand had handed the cheque to her and she'd noticed his signature, and the fact it was a personal cheque, she had tried to argue, convinced the cheque should be drawn on the estate of Carlos Diez. But Rand had dismissed her concern, stating as executor it was perfectly acceptable for the money to be paid out of his account, because he would recoup all expenses when the estate was settled.

She had signed the document giving him the option to buy her share, which she thought was a bit pointless as she had no intention of marrying him. But if it kept him happy she didn't mind. Though she still was not happy about the money coming directly from Rand, but she was in no position to argue, she needed the cash quickly. Sighing, Jules stood up and, walking across to the dressing table, she picked up her purse and slid the cheque inside. She had got what she wanted so why worry? she told herself firmly.

The future looked better and the present wasn't half bad; most women would kill for a few days in the company of Rand Carducci. Jules grinned as she pulled off her shirt, stepped out of her jeans and padded across the room to the *en suite* bathroom. She needed a wash and change before meeting him for dinner. It was pathetic really, but for once she wished she had something glamorous to wear instead of the suit she had arrived in.

Ten minutes later she eyed the green silk knit dress she had discovered in the closet and thought, Not bad. Made for ease of travelling, it was a simple shift with a crew neck and no sleeves. She slipped her feet back into her high-heeled sandals, and fastened a gold link belt, another find, loosely around her slender waist. She pushed her hair casually behind her ears, and left it to fall in a cascade of curls down past her shoulder blades. Jules straightened her shoulders, made her way downstairs and walked into the main sitting room.

'You look stunning.'

Jules pivoted around on her heel to see Rand standing beside the drinks cabinet half concealed by the open door. 'This old thing?' she tried to joke, but even to her own ears she sounded breathless. And why not? She almost groaned. Her mesmerised eyes roved from his dark head, over the great body now clad in a casual-styled cream linen suit, to the softly gleaming leather of his handmade shoes, and back up again.

He slowly shook his head. 'If that is an old thing,' he murmured huskily, his eyes roaming over her slender body with blatant masculine appraisal, 'then God help me if you ever wear a designer gown.'

'Flatterer,' she mocked, totally unaware that the loose shift she had thought simple clung to her breasts and hips in a way it never had when she was seventeen.

'I need a drink,' Rand said with a chuckle. 'What will you have, Jules? Champagne to celebrate our successful negotiations?'

'Yes, please.' Why not? Jules thought recklessly. She had got what she came for, and it felt as if a weight had lifted from her shoulders. Her mother was going to have the best treatment money could buy, and she felt like celebrating.

# CHAPTER FIVE

JULES, with a half-empty glass of champagne in her hand, sank back in the soft-cushioned sofa and sighed with contentment. It was the best meal she had had in months, and when Donna entered the sitting room to ask if they wanted any more coffee Jules told her so. Though her enjoyment of the meal could have had something to do with the fact that at last she could face the immediate future with a lot more hope and a lot less worry.

'You look a bit like the cat that got the cream,' Rand remarked, standing in front of her with a half-smile of considerable warmth on his rugged face and a bottle of champagne in one hand. 'Or perhaps a red fox,' he teased, reaching and tucking some errant strands of her long hair back behind her ear. 'You are one very foxy lady.'

'Dark auburn, if you please,' Jules teased back, colouring ever so slightly, and trying to ignore his last complimentary comment, while secretly pleased.

Their business finally settled to their mutual satisfaction, dinner had been a convivial affair. Rand, she had discovered, was a great conversationalist. They had discussed music, the theatre. He was a lover of opera, which was hardly surprising given he was Italian, and he had laughed at her confession she was an ardent horror-movie fan. They shared much the same taste in books, both having a preference for biographies, with Jules confessing again she also had a passion for romances.

'Oh, you do please me.'

His husky-voiced comment and his finger lingering in the hollow between her throat and shoulder cut through her musings in a purely physical way. Her mouth suddenly dry, she glanced up at him and wondered how she had ever thought he was old and cold. He had removed his jacket after dinner, and his tailored silk shirt revealed the musculature of his upper body to perfection. Her heart gave a strange little flutter and she could do nothing about the suddenly racing pulse in her slender neck.

Her expressive features gave her away. Rand guessed exactly where her thoughts were leading and his dark eyes gleamed with a sensual satisfaction as he added with deliberate provocation, 'You please me in every way, though some we have yet to explore.'

Jules felt the heat creeping up her cheeks, but she tried to counter cheekily, 'In your dreams!'

'Well, maybe not yet,' Rand conceded. 'First let's finish the champagne.' And before she could refuse he had filled her glass, then his own, and, placing the empty bottle on the sofa table, lowered himself down beside her.

'I don't usually drink,' Jules blurted, 'but as it's a celebration...' She felt the lightest pressure of his thigh against hers, unintentional, she told herself, but suddenly she was nervous again and took a gulp of champagne. 'And Donna did make a marvellous meal,' she babbled on—whether it was the alcohol or the close proximity of Rand's virile, masculine body so close to her own that affected her, she wasn't sure. 'I was so relieved when I arrived and her and Sanchez welcomed me with open arms. I was afraid they might be angry that I had never visited before now, the funeral and everything.'

'It would hardly have been surprising if they had.' Rand put down his glass and, turning slightly, slanted her a sardonic glance. 'Considering they have to wait six months to find out if they still have a home. But luckily for you they both adore you and this evening I was able to reassure them that their jobs were safe.'

'Wait a minute!' Jules exclaimed, appalled by his implication. 'Tell me they weren't waiting for me?' she demanded, her emerald-green eyes flashing reproach. 'Surely you could have told them they had nothing to worry about?' She plonked her empty glass on the table. 'You are the executor, for heaven's sake.'

One broad shoulder elevated in a shrug. 'But of course they were waiting for you—we all were. No decision could be made until you had arrived and read the codicil and, strictly speaking, the six months were almost up.'

'But either way you could have told them you would keep them on, whatever.'

'I was in no position to give them that guarantee.' Rand's dark eyes narrowed on her and once again he was the intimidating, remote businessman she remembered. 'You could have decided to fulfil your father's wish, and demanded we marry. Lived here for a year and then sold your half to anybody, and they might still end up homeless. But now you have settled on what you want, plus even if you change your mind I have the option to buy your share. I was able to reassure Sanchez, Donna and all the staff.'

'Oh, my God!' Jules got to her feet. 'I must go and apologise to Donna. I had no idea, and her pregnant! I never thought... I feel awful.' Her voice rose sharply on the last word, and cracked on the sob choking her throat. She had been so tied up in her mother's illness and her own money problem; it had never once entered her head to consider anyone else.

'Wait.' Rand stood up and reached for her; she looked up at him, her green eyes hazed with moisture. 'You silly fool, it is not your fault.' He hauled her close, muttering some imprecation in his own language. 'If it was anyone's fault it was your father's, with the codicil and the six-month deadline. Or blame me—I should never have agreed to go along with it.'

She wrapped her arms around his waist and clung as the tears trickled down over her cheeks. She didn't consider herself an emotional person, and she didn't know why she was crying—for her father, her mother, or simply as a release from the tension of the past few months—but she was ashamed of her weakness.

'Please don't cry.' Rand's husky-voiced plea was whispered against her ear. 'I can't bear to see you cry.' He tipped her chin up with one long finger. 'Everything is fine.'

Jules looked at him with wide, wet eyes and suddenly she was aware of a host of more earthy emotions; the warmth, the power of his body, his arm supporting her. The beginnings of a blue shadow on his square jaw, the sensuous curve of his lips, the tide of colour along his high cheekbones. 'I've embarrassed you, by crying. I'm sorry,' she whispered, feeling thoroughly ashamed at her own behaviour.

'No. It is not embarrassment I am suffering from,' Rand said roughly, his arm tightening around her waist. 'It is something much more basic,' he declared huskily, his glittering eyes burning down into hers.

She felt the fierce tension in every powerful inch of his large, lithe body, her pelvis in intimate contact with the thrusting strength of his very masculine arousal. And the sudden and totally shocking responding surge of awareness through every cell in her own body took her breath away.

'I know,' she breathed honestly. Suddenly the physical world of sexual temptation, a world she had thought herself immune to, invaded her mind and she trembled with the sheer power of what she was feeling. Their eyes met, black luring green, an explicit question asked and agreed between them without a word being spoken.

'Jules.' He said her name and moved with a speed that overwhelmed her. His hand raked through the tangled mass of her hair, his other moved down over her bottom, hauling her harder against him as his mouth captured hers with a fierce, devouring passion that made any last-minute thought of resistance laughable... Not that she wanted to...

She returned the kiss with a wild, wondering innocence, her tongue darting greedily for more.

'*Dio.*' He groaned, his mouth gentling on hers. 'Not here.' Raising his head, he lifted her in his arms.

Jules wrapped an arm around his neck and clung. She reached a finger to trace the firm shape of his jaw, the slight indentation in the centre, not quite a dimple, and a slow smile curved her lips. She looked at him with darkened emerald eyes full of sensual anticipation that she could not disguise. For the first time in her life she was prepared to take the risk and let her emotions rule. She might regret it in the morning, but she no longer cared; the feelings Rand aroused were so intense that they consumed her to the exclusion of everything else. All she wanted, all she needed was promised in the incandescent gleam in his jet-black eyes.

'You are sure?' Rand groaned a few minutes later as he lowered her slowly down the long length of his body to the floor.

She vaguely noticed it was her old bedroom before his hands tightened on her shoulders and he moved her back to an arm-length away. His dark eyes roaming avidly over her shapely body, lingering on the proud jut of her breasts beneath the clinging fabric of her dress. 'Because, *amore*, once I start I cannot promise to stop. I am no saint.'

She didn't want a saint; she wanted this sinfully sexy man to take her to bed. The strength of her feelings was so intense they overruled her normal morality, her basically shy nature, with an avid curiosity to explore to the ultimate degree what Rand was offering.

'I have never been more sure of anything in my life,' Jules whispered, and she placed her hands on his chest, her fingers finding the buttons of his shirt, and slowly she began to release them, exposing his naked torso to her view.

'Oh, my,' she breathed, fascinated by the bronzed muscular chest, her fingers tracing over soft, curling body hair, accidentally catching a pebble-like nipple. She felt his great body shudder and hesitated for a moment, looking up into his blazing eyes, and her pale skin burned under the intensity of his arrested gaze.

'Don't stop now, Jules.' Rand groaned. He was dominant by nature and preferred to be dominant in bed, but he had never felt anything so erotic as Jules' slender fingers caressing his flesh with a delicate curiosity that made every inch of his powerful body quiver with the raw force of his tension.

Jules smoothed the black curls of hair and deliberately traced the shape of the hard, dark nipples with gentle fascination, before letting her hands slide higher beneath the silk and slip his shirt slowly from his broad shoulders, her whole body trembling with excitement and amazement at her own daring.

'*Dio mio!*' he groaned in Italian and, moving with an abruptness that shocked her, he dragged her into his arms and closed his mouth in fierce, possessive passion over hers. He snatched the initiative from her as he invaded the moist interior of her mouth, his tongue a probing masculine imitation of the most intimate penetration possible.

She clung to him, her slender body vibrating like a stringed instrument at the touch of a master, all her senses leaping into heated automatic response as he unleashed the full force of his desire on her. It was no gentle seduction but a fiery introduction to what was to follow.

'You are so beautiful,' Rand husked when he allowed her to breathe again. 'Let me look at you.' And in a moment her dress and bra were on the floor and his trousers had joined them.

Jules was left standing before him wearing only white lace briefs. Some faint shred of modesty made her attempt to fold her arms over her breasts. But he took her mouth again and bit gently on her bottom lip before kissing her with a deep, hungry passion that had her drowning mindlessly in a sea of sensations that she had never before dreamt existed.

'You cannot be shy before me.' Rand groaned, and, lifting his dark head, he caught her wrists and held her arms wide, baring her breasts, and the creamy mounds swelled in shameless response to his heated appraisal.

'Exquisite does not do you justice.' He reached for her slender shoulders, traced the hollow of her collar-bone and trailed slowly down to cup her sensitive breasts with firm hands. A flush of pink swept from her toes to the top of her head in a total body blush.

'Amazing.' Rand husked. 'You still blush.'

*Still blush.* A faint thread of sanity registered the words, but Jules shrank from the connotation, too lost in the wonder of Rand. His thumbs stroked her rosy pink nipples, teasing the sensitised tips, and she gasped out loud.

He bent his dark head and kissed her again, before he lifted her and laid her on the bed. She watched him shamelessly as he discarded his boxer shorts, and the blush went from pink to scarlet. He was broad, tall and naked, and for a second a brief flicker of virginal fear widened her deep green eyes at the sight of his magnificently aroused masculinity.

But he bent over her and kissed her again, and she forgot her fear, she forgot everything but the man overshadowing her. His hand curved her waist, his long fingers easing beneath the top of her briefs, his fingers soothing over the quivering tautness of her stomach and thighs as he removed her one remaining garment before he joined her on the bed.

He leant on one elbow and looked down at her in a long, lingering scrutiny, and he chuckled. 'Definitely red, Jules.' Whether he was referring to her blushing or something more intimate, she did not know and she did not care.

He bent his head, the tip of his tongue licking around the outline of her lips, and just when she thought he was going to kiss her again his head dipped lower and his tongue licked down the valley between her breasts. She reached for him, her small hands curving over his broad shoulders, and digging into the satin-smooth flesh as his tongue swept up and over one firm breast and laved the tight rosy nipple. A soft moan escaped her, and accentuated into a cry at the exquisite torture as he sucked the engorged tip into his mouth. Her back arched, and her hands swept up into his hair, holding him to her, wanting the erotic torment to go on and on.

Her blood flowed hot and thick through her veins and restlessly she moved beneath him, urging him to deliver the same fierce pleasures to her other breast, and she groaned her delight when he obliged.

'You like that, Jules.' He glanced up at her with smouldering black eyes and chuckled softly, then covered her mouth again, nipping and teasing, licking and probing with a devastating expertise.

Helplessly she writhed against him, her hips lifting, intensely aware of the brush of skin on skin. The erotic torment of his hand sliding down over her breast, the curve of her waist, the tautness of her stomach before finding the tangle of curls at the apex of her thighs. Jules' whole body jerked out of control, her thighs involuntarily parting, anticipating a much deeper invasion.

Long fingers stroked the hot, damp warmth revealed with a tactile expertise that made her whimper with the fierce heat of sexual tension, even as his head swooped down and she felt again the erotic tug of his mouth on her nipples. She was lost in the throes of some incredible passion she had never imagined in her wildest dreams. Her hands of their own volition stroked and caressed down his back, traced his spine, the curve of his buttock, around to the hollow of hip and thigh and daringly touched his aroused flesh. His great body shuddered and his head jerked up and he ravished her swollen lips once more.

'Rand.' She groaned his name as he shifted over her, and she lifted her hips, burning up in the fiery excitement, and tortured by the need, the ache for the final fulfilment.

'*Sí, amore,*' he grated, and swiftly drew her up to him and plunged deep inside her. Her eyes flew wide in shock as a fierce pain lanced through her, and she drew in her breath on a cry.

'*No credibile.*' His smouldering eyes held her, and his great body stilled, his rugged features clenching, a tide of dark colour scarring his high cheekbones as he fought for control.

The pain subsiding, she saw the shock in his eyes and, terrified he was going to stop when she was so close to discovering the ultimate joy of his possession with an instinct as old as time, she wrapped her long legs around him. She felt his great body tremble, and the force of his own desire broke his rigid control and he drove deeper still inside her.

The pain vanished as if it had never been as he stilled for a moment. Heat and tension flooded through her as he slowly withdrew. She reached and pressed her lips to his throat, his shoulder, her hand curving around the nape of his neck, and she gasped her relief as he surged into her again.

She cried out his name as his hands grasped the back of her hips and he moved inside her, driving her higher and higher. The blood pounded through her veins and the wet, slick heat of his mighty body both inside and out drove her with shattering intensity to a pitch of excitement beyond pleasure almost to pain, before she went over the edge in an explosion of convulsing release.

Jules felt his great body shudder and his hoarse cry, and she clung to him as he joined her in the swirling darkness that overwhelmed her.

'Jules. Jules.' She opened dazed eyes and focused on his dark face. 'Are you okay?' She felt his swift withdrawal and quickly reassured him.

'Never better,' she said on a shaky breath, her lips parting in an ecstatic smile. At last she had found a man she could give herself to with all the pent-up passion and generosity of her loving nature. But her smile was not returned as Rand dragged himself free of her arms and rolled off her to lie flat on his back.

'Will you still be saying that in a month, I wonder?' he said mockingly.

'For as long as you want me to,' Jules replied, still caught up in the euphoria of their lovemaking; she slid her arm across his taut stomach and snuggled closer to his side with a contented sigh.

Abruptly her arm was thrown off him and he surged up to lean over her. 'Are you crazy? Why the hell did you not tell me you were a virgin?' he demanded, the lover of a few moments ago unrecognisable in the snarling man staring down at her.

'You never asked. Does it matter?' Something was very wrong, and the languorous feeling of complete satisfaction was fading fast beneath the angry eyes of her lover.

'I never asked.' Rand flung the words back at her. 'Look at you.' His eyes swept down over her naked body and back to her face. 'You have a body to put Marilyn Monroe to shame and you're what? Twenty-four -five? No man in the world would look at you and think for a minute you were a virgin. For God's sake, you were engaged!'

'I don't get your point,' Jules said blankly. 'You're mad because you were my first lover?'

'No,' Rand yelled, 'I'm mad because you could be pregnant.' He leapt off the bed, and stood glowering down at her.

'Oh, I see.' Jules sat up and pulled the cover over her body. Feeling a bit as if she had just plunged naked into the Arctic Ocean as every lingering pleasurable sensation vanished beneath his unexpected onslaught. But at least he did not regret being her first lover if his adamant 'No' was to be believed. She supposed she should be thankful for small mercies, or not small at all in Rand's case, even with his manhood quiescent, the errant naughty thought impinged on her shock at his outburst.

But his attitude was a starkly painful reality check. While she was deluding herself that this might finally be love, he was angry that she might be pregnant. Rand could not have made it plainer if he tried that he was only looking for a one-night stand, or a brief affair at best.

A week in Chile, and Jules was getting chillier by the second… She could set his mind at rest, but suddenly she was not just hurt, she was furious. Call her *crazy,* would he? He should have been controlling his own impulses, the arrogant pig.

Lifting her head, she looked up into his hard dark features. 'So it is all my fault,' she prompted, her green eyes shooting sparks. 'You're a sexually active mature male—where were your brains half an hour ago?' she demanded mockingly, glancing pointedly down his great body and back to his face. She heard his sharp intake of breath, and knew it was not the meek response he had been expecting. 'Or need I ask?' she derided.

Rand Carducci, for the only time in his adult life, found himself struck dumb and embarrassed in front of a lover in the bedroom…

Jules sat there, a thin sheet covering her luscious breasts, her head tilted back revealing the elegant sweep of her swan-like neck, her brilliant emerald eyes staring defiantly into his. She was stunningly beautiful, with her long hair tumbled around her shoulders in magnificent disarray, a disarray he was responsible for, along with everything else, he was forced to admit. She was right, damn her! He was meticulous in his relationships with women and never forgot to use a condom. It was only the bewitching woman before him who addled his brain. But why? his mind finally questioned, then he remembered her earlier comment that a wealthy international businessman could not hang around, and suddenly he realised he had fallen for the oldest trick in the book.

'I might have been thinking below the waist but you sure as hell weren't,' Rand drawled scathingly. 'I believed I was making love to a sexually active woman. I don't do virgins.' A bitter, cynical smile curled his firm lips. 'But then you knew that, Jules—why else would you come on to me like a whore, stripping my shirt from my body?' he demanded with chilling hostility.

Like a whore! 'I did not.' Jules was horrified and hurting at the picture he painted of her innocent attempt to please him.

'Don't bother to deny it. I have got your number. The adamant denial you didn't want to spend a year here to get your share of the ranch. The small amount you were prepared to settle for, the sweet smiles—I thought you were too good to be true and I was right. How much easier for you to get yourself pregnant by an extremely wealthy man, and run back home to England to live in comfort with an income guaranteed for years. Talk about like mother like daughter...' he said with cold derision. 'Well, I hate to tell you that you picked the wrong man. I am no Carlos Diez... If there is any repercussion from tonight, I will keep the child, and you will get nothing. I'll tie you up in the law courts for so long you will wish you had never set eyes on me.'

'I already do,' Jules whispered, slowly shaking her head, unable to believe what she was hearing. His crack about her mother was doubly hurtful. Rand actually thought she had deliberately set out to trap him into making her pregnant, and yet not so long ago he had been making love to her with a magnificent passion that had melted her bones.

'You and I both,' he snarled. 'I do not appreciate being taken for a fool and a meal ticket.'

That was it. Jules had had enough. The man had to be crazy, and even though she felt as if her heart had been sliced into a million pieces her pride and anger came to the fore and she began to fight back.

'You must be deranged, and I wouldn't have your child if you were the last man on earth.'

'You would terminate my child?' he demanded incredulously.

Her chaotic emotions in turmoil, all of a sudden Jules had a hysterical desire to laugh. She had made an amazing discovery. Rand the cold, remote businessman was anything but when his passions were aroused. He was as volatile as nitroglycerine, with an all-too-vivid imagination. He had gone from yelling at her for being a virgin, to blaming her for trying to get pregnant, and now he was shocked at the thought she might terminate his child, all in the space of a few minutes.

'No, Rand,' she said softly. He didn't deserve her consideration after what he had just called her, but she wanted to put an end to this pointless argument and escape to lick her wounds in peace.

'But you have nothing to worry about,' she continued. He was staring at her with an angry intensity, and something more that unbelievably sent her pulse racing all over again. 'I promise.' She waved a dismissive hand in his direction and slipped off the other side of the bed, dragging the sheet with her. 'I need a shower.' What she really needed was to get away before she succumbed yet again to the high-octane level of physical awareness that she felt anywhere near him.

'Wait,' Rand commanded harshly. 'I am not finished talking to you.'

Jules stopped at the entrance to the *en suite* and glanced over her shoulder. He was walking around the bed. 'Relax, Rand, I am on the pill.' The look on his face was priceless, but Jules did not stop to savour the moment. She ducked into the bathroom, slamming the door behind her and shooting the bolt.

A fist thundered on the door. 'What did you say? How can you be? And open this damn door.'

She could hear the incredulity in his tone, and she shrank back against the vanity unit; she would not have put it past him to break in.

'I told you—I am on the pill on doctor's orders, have been for three months,' she yelled back. It was the truth. When her mother had been diagnosed with cancer Jules' periods had become irregular. Her doctor had said it was quite a common occurrence after a big emotional shock and a few months on the pill would regulate them again. 'So you can stop worrying and go count your assets and leave me the hell alone.'

To her astonishment she heard a shout of laughter. 'Enjoy your shower.' A light tap on the door followed. 'I'll catch you later.' And then silence.

# CHAPTER SIX

HE DIDN'T have to sound so relieved, Jules thought bitterly, letting the sheet drop to the floor. It would have served the devil right if she had been after him for his money. After all, Rand was the man who said he was willing to marry her for convenience. He had obviously lied if his reaction a moment ago was to be believed, and, turning, she looked at her reflection in the vanity mirror.

She barely recognised herself in the wide-eyed woman that stared back. The swollen contours of her mouth were testament to the hungry kisses they had shared; she licked her lips, and she could still taste Rand on her tongue.

She lowered her eyes and inexplicably they flooded with tears as she spotted the slight reddish marks on her breasts, and she stumbled back a pace, stunned as the realisation of what had happened hit her.

She saw the imprint of his fingers on her thighs. 'Oh, my God, how could I have been so stupid?' she groaned out loud, drowning in shame and humiliation at the enormity of what she had done by giving herself to a man like Rand, who cared nothing for her.

When she had imagined losing her virginity she had dreamt of softly murmured words of love, and romance, the meeting of two souls. Instead she had thrown it away on Rand Carducci with all the wanton eagerness of a nymphomaniac, and she felt sick to her stomach.

Choking back a sob, Jules turned away from the mirror and stumbled into the shower stall. The most demeaning thing of all, she sadly acknowledged, was that her body was still hot and aching with the memory of their wild, wonderful passion and she had the awful conviction that with very little encouragement she would do the same thing again, the image of his magnificent naked body flashing through her brain and heating her flesh.

Frantically fumbling, she activated the cold-water tap and tensed as the icy spray hit her, but slowly it served its purpose: the heat, her hunger for the man, subsided. When she started to shiver she turned on the mixer and flung back her head and let the warm, soothing spray wash over her for a moment. Finally she picked up the soap and began to scrub her tender flesh, determined to remove any trace of his touch from her body. Stepping out of the shower, she picked up a towel and swiftly dried her body, and tried to tell herself she had succeeded.

So she had lost her senses and her virginity to Rand, a man who did not value either very much, it would seem, and she had only herself to blame. What had she expected? A declaration of undying love! Who was she kidding? Herself, that was whom, she recognised bitterly… It had been lust plain and simple, and she could not believe that she had succumbed so quickly, so easily to the most basic of human emotions.

Half an hour later, her hair washed and dried and with a large white bath sheet wrapped around her, toga-style, she pressed her ear to the door. There wasn't a sound to be heard. Rand must be long gone, but even so she was reluctant to open the door. She could not bear to face him, to see the sensual knowledge in his eyes as he looked at her. It was childish, she knew, but she could not help it.

Mortified at her own weakness, she flung open the door and marched into the bedroom. It was empty, and, looking at the rumpled bed, she sighed. The scene of her downfall, she thought, her eyes filling with tears. She brushed them away with the back of her hand, and, crossing to the bed, decided there was no alternative. She dropped the towel and crawled under the cover, physically and emotionally exhausted.

She was leaving here tomorrow and she was never coming back; her mind was made up. This place and the people associated with it had caused her nothing but heartbreak. It was time to draw a line under the whole sorry mess.

Jules rolled over in the bed. The scent of Rand lingered on the sheet and a few more tears rolled down her cheeks. Fiercely she brushed them away; self-pity was a destructive emotion she refused to succumb to.

She was twenty-five, for heaven's sake, not some starry-eyed teenager. So she had finally had sex with a man—it was no big deal. In fact some would say it was way past time... Jules just had to convince herself she believed it.

In the meantime she consoled herself with the thought that she had her health and strength and the money she needed—she did not need Rand Carducci.

Jules looked out of her bedroom window and saw Sanchez stroll down towards the stables. The working day had started. She glanced at her wrist-watch: seven a.m. Time to be going. She straightened the bottom of her jacket and picked up her purse, and then, swinging on her heel, she left the room. She didn't look back but walked downstairs, her high heels clicking on the tiled floor.

After a restless night she had given up trying to sleep altogether at five in the morning. She had roamed around the room, checking all the drawers and closets, but there was nothing she wanted to take with her. Her life, what little had been, here in Chile was well and truly over. She had even managed to smile at the over-the-top frilly wedding dress, and wondered how she had ever been so naive.

She had one more thing to do, she realised as she pushed open the kitchen door and walked in.

'Julia.' Donna turned from the stove where she was preparing breakfast. 'I was going to bring your coffee up, but Señor Rand said to let you sleep.'

'Kind of him, but not necessary, Donna, and don't worry, just give me a cup of your wonderful coffee, and I will be on my way.'

'You're leaving.' The housekeeper's eyes widened in shock. 'But Señor Rand said you were staying a week.'

'Yes, well, he was wrong.' Walking across the kitchen, Jules dropped her purse on the table and accepted the cup of coffee Donna held out to her. She pulled out a chair and sat down at the large scrubbed wooden table. 'I have to get back home. My mother needs me; she is not too well.' She glanced up at the housekeeper. 'But come and share a coffee with me before I leave,' she suggested.

Donna filled a cup and sat down at the opposite side of the table, her brown eyes, sad

and wise, fixed on Jules. 'We were all saddened by the death of your father, but he had
passed the seventy years the Lord allows. But
I remember your mother; she was so young
and so beautiful. I hope it is nothing serious.'

A smile tinged with sadness tilted the corners of Jules' mouth. 'It was quite serious, but
thankfully she is recovering well,' she said
lightly. 'But we do have a business to run and
I need to get back to help.' And for the next
ten minutes she told Donna all about the bakery and her expansion into corporate catering,
her life in England, finally ending with, 'I am
pleased Rand has managed to set your mind at
rest about the ranch, Donna. If I had known
you were worried I would have come much
sooner and settled things. But now it is all
over.' Jules got to her feet and walked around
to Donna and hugged her shoulders. 'It will be
nice to think of you and Sanchez, being here
where you truly belong, and with a child.' She
patted Donna's stomach gently. 'I am really
delighted for you. But now I must go.' She
straightened up.

'Go where?' Rand's deep voice demanded
curtly.

Jules turned slowly, the sound of his voice throwing her hard-won self-control into utter confusion. He had entered from the yard, and her heart missed a beat at the sight of him. He was wearing white running shorts and a vest, the lot plastered to him with sweat, his mighty chest heaving from his exertions. 'You've been running,' she said inanely. Now she knew how he kept his magnificent physique.

'I do every day.' He brushed a hand through his sweat-damp hair, and her green eyes clashed with the density of Rand's flashing gaze and she swallowed hard. 'But you have not answered my question.' His eyes raked over her, noting the glorious red hair swept back in a braid, the linen suit, and the high-heeled sandals. She certainly was not dressed for hanging around the ranch. 'Where do you think you are going?' He strode towards her, stopping only inches from her face.

Her stomach turned over. The hot, musky scent of him teased her nostrils—he was a very virile male, a very scantily clad virile male, and only last night she had been a very willing female body in his bed. She blinked away the seductive memory, and told herself she was just one of many as he had so succinctly told her when he had discovered he was her first lover. He was used to a string of sophisticated, sexually mature females and he had assumed she was one.

Squaring her shoulders, she looked at him. 'I am going home today if I can change my flight. Our business is settled, and there is no reason for me to stay,' she said flatly.

A hand suddenly closed tightly around her wrist. 'Jules is a bit confused.' Rand slanted a brief smile at Donna, sitting wide-eyed and watching. 'Be an angel and serve coffee in the study.'

'Let go of me.' Jules tried to tug her arm free, but to no avail as without a word he dragged her with him out into the hall, and with a hand at her back pushed her into the study.

'Now what do you think you are playing at, Jules?' he demanded tautly. 'We have a deal, you and I.'

Keeping a few feet of space between them, she had to force herself to look at him again and remain calm. 'Yes, and I am going to stick to it; you have nothing to worry about,' she said stiffly.

He had gone very still, his hooded dark eyes were fixed on her with an intensity that sent a sliver of fear down her spine, and it took every atom of will-power she possessed to carry on. 'But I see no reason to spend any more time here. My father is dead—it can make no difference to him whether I am here or not,' she offered firmly, but inside she was a quivering mess. 'And I am needed at home.'

'You are needed here,' Rand murmured coolly. 'You promised to stay a week and I am holding you to that.' His strong face was taut and his eyes gleamed with a light that was anything but cool as his gaze raked over her shapely curves and back to her face, and his hand reached out to snare her waist, but she twisted hastily away from his arm.

'For my father's sake, of course.' She arched one delicate brow in cynical disbelief. She could see it in his eyes, feel it in the air, in the shimmering tension that arced between them. He wanted sex, no-strings sex, while he was stuck here for a few days tying up the affairs of the ranch, and after last night he knew she was available.

He had called her little better than a whore and declared she was after *his* money, and when she had proved him wrong he had laughed… Yet looking at him now she still wanted him. But, calling up every bit of pride she possessed, she added, 'Well, sorry, but it is impossible.' Turning, unable to stand his intense appraisal any longer without clawing his eyes out for the arrogant devil he was, she walked across to the display of trophies on one wall.

'But before I leave I would like to take a token home for my mother.' In the lonely hour before dawn it had suddenly hit her that unless she took something back to show her mother she would have to admit it was money she'd been after all along and why. Her mother was a very proud woman, and Jules knew if she told her the truth her mum was quite likely to refuse the money.

Her eyes skated over the array of trophies on the mahogany shelves and she picked up the one her father had won in England the year her parents had met. 'This would be appropriate.' She turned around and suddenly Rand's face was once again only inches from hers. Nervously she licked her suddenly dry lips with the tip of her tongue, her heart rate accelerating in her chest, as if it were her who had been out running.

'What would be appropriate, *amore*, is for you to stop lying to me and yourself,' he said silkily, his hand closing over hers holding the trophy. 'You want me as badly as I want you.' His other hand lifted to curve around her neck. 'I can feel the pulse pounding in your throat, and I can remember in every vivid detail the way your body welcomed mine, the way your legs wrapped around my waist refusing to let me go.'

Heat scorched up her face and she was ashamed of her body's traitorous reaction. 'Shut up...just shut up...' she cried and, flinging off his hand holding hers, she would have crowned him with the silver-mounted trophy, but he was too quick for her. He gripped her wrist and twisted it around her back, the trophy falling from her nerveless fingers to clatter on the floor.

'Really, Jules, violence…you do surprise me,' he mocked, pulling her towards his hard body. 'But keep it for the bedroom,' and he kissed her.

She tore her mouth away from his and with her one free hand she tried to push him away, but he simply caught both her hands behind her back and hauled her hard against him. She tossed her head from side to side, but his mouth found her throat, and tasted her skin. Needle pricks of pleasure darted through her flesh, alerting every sensual nerve in her body. She struggled wildly against him, lifting a knee, her intention plain.

'Oh, no, you don't, you little wild cat,' Rand growled and for a second she was free before she found her back against the wall and Rand's hands clasping her upper arms holding her firm, while his long legs trapped her slender hips in the curve of his pelvis, making her blatantly aware of his aroused state.

She looked up at him with furious green eyes, her heart pounding like a wild thing in her breast. 'Get off me, you great brute. Or I'll scream.' She could not move and she was more frightened of herself than him. She could feel the pressure of every muscle and sinew of his large body from her chest to her thighs, and her traitorous body ached to melt against him.

'By all accounts women who warn they are going to scream never do,' he said mockingly, his dark eyes gleaming with a devilish light down into hers.

Infuriated beyond belief by his arrogant assumption, Jules opened her mouth and the crushing force of Rand's mouth on hers choked off the scream. He took full advantage of her parted lips, his tongue thrusting into the hot interior with a wicked expertise that in moments had her accepting and finally responding with a shaming urgency that she could no longer control. It wasn't fair, her mind screamed a denial, but it was, oh, so good! her body answered.

'No more arguments,' Rand murmured against her pouting lips, a long moment later. 'You will stay as planned.'

Jules looked up into his dark face, saw the passion smouldering in his eyes, and opened her mouth to agree, but she caught the flicker of triumph in the glittering black depths and suddenly she was appalled at her own weak surrender. One kiss and he thought she was his, and the conceit of the man made her temperature rise, not with desire but with a slow-burning anger.

'You called me a whore.' He had no idea how his words had hurt her last night, and what was more he didn't care... 'And that I was after your money.'

Rand groaned. 'I can't believe I said that,' he confessed huskily, and, cupping her head between his two hands, he gently tilted her face up to his. 'You must know I didn't mean it. How could I? I had just discovered you were a virgin. My only excuse for shouting at you the way I did was shock.'

'Shock,' she repeated, staring incredulously. If anyone had a reason to be shocked it was Jules, making love for the first time. For a man of Rand's age and experience it had to be pretty commonplace.

'Yes.' He dropped his hands to her shoulders and then down to curve his arms loosely around her back, putting a little space between them. 'I admit I am cynical by nature, and it seemed too incredible to believe that you would give yourself to me and not want anything in return.' As she watched she saw an arrested expression darken his harshly attractive face. 'Tell me—why did you, Jules?'

With a swift push she ducked out of his arms and moved to the centre of the room. It was the one question she could not answer.

'Jules…?' He came up behind her, and she spun around to face him like a deer held at bay in the sights of the hunter.

'Coming back to this house…emotional overload…too much champagne…jet lag or just plain lust… Take your pick?' Her green eyes flashed him a defiant glance, and she ignored his sudden stillness and the tightening of his sensual mouth and added, 'But it sure as hell was not to get myself pregnant and earn a few pounds, and I am certainly not staying here.'

'So I misjudged you last night,' he conceded harshly. 'But that is no reason for you to run away this morning.'

Jules saw the barely leashed fury in his black eyes, and tore her gaze from his to study her feet. 'I am not running away—' she emphasised each word '—I am leaving.' She spied the trophy lying on the floor and, dipping down, she retrieved it. She caught a movement in the corner of her eye and a pair of scuffed trainers and long, tanned, muscular legs filled her vision as she slowly straightened up.

Rand was still as a statue. His hooded dark eyes, fringed with ebony lashes, stared at her with probing intensity. She smoothed her skirt down over her hip with a damp palm, clutching the trophy tightly in her other hand.

Jules took a step back. 'So if that is all…' she tried for a smile that did not quite come off '…I will get Sanchez to run me back to town.'

'Yes. Sure, if that is what you want.' Rand shrugged his broad shoulders as if he couldn't care less, and smoothly turned his dark head as the study door opened and Donna walked in with the coffee.

Jules watched him in disbelief. She had forgotten all about Donna and the coffee in the turmoil of the past few minutes, but Rand had not. Rand was cool. Rand was in total control. He spoke to Donna, the tray was deposited on the desk and Donna left. Jules had been worrying about nothing; Rand did not give a fig what she did. It was her own stupid heart that was involved, not his. 'I won't bother with coffee. I'm going to find Sanchez,' she said flatly, and headed for the door.

'You do that, so long as you understand the cheque will not be honoured if you leave today.'

Her hand was reaching for the door handle when she heard his words; she let it fall to her side and slowly straightened up to her full height. Shock held her rigid. Was Rand really that ruthless? She took a few deep steadying breaths and squared her slender shoulders. 'You would do that?' she asked quietly, her back to him. She didn't trust herself to look at Rand, not without launching the trophy in her hand at his arrogant head.

'Yes. I am a businessman, I don't allow anyone to renege on any part of a deal after it is agreed and that includes you, Jules,' he declared bluntly. 'I don't bend my rules even for a lover.'

Rand saw her shoulders stiffen, and cursed under his breath. He was handling Jules all wrong, and it was so unlike him. But then she had been one damn shock after another. A heartless girl who never turned up for her own father's funeral, and when eventually she did turn up wanted money—that he could understand. But the innocent woman who gave her body to him last night and didn't want his money—he still could not get his head around that yet. He couldn't fathom what made Jules tick, and experience had taught him never to accept a woman at face value.

Jules owed him big time and he wanted to dislike her, but instead his body sizzled when he got within a few feet of her. Hell, she only had to be in the same room and he was as hard as a rock, and that had never happened to him before.

His expression darkened as he eyed her slender back. He didn't need to blackmail a woman into his bed; usually they were fighting for the privilege. Who the hell did she think she was to walk out on him?

Very slowly Jules turned back to face him. 'Okay, I will stay.' She needed the money; she had no option.

'Great. I knew you would be reasonable.' Rand stepped forward, his sensuous mouth quirking at the corners in the beginnings of a smile. Perhaps Jules was simply not a morning person, he rationalised, and that was probably what made her cranky. 'Now come and join me in a coffee and we can forget our little disagreement, and discuss what to do with the rest of the day.'

She saw his hand lift and neatly sidestepped out of his way. Jules couldn't believe she had been such a fool as to give herself to a man who did not know her at all. Rand had all the sensitivity, the emotional depths of a hammer-head shark, and he was just as dense and just as lethal. Coming over all sweetness and light because he thought he had got his own way. What a jerk!

She looked at him with ice-green eyes. 'There is no need for a discussion; if I am to keep my side of the deal then you must keep yours. As it is obvious we don't trust each other, we will go to Santiago and I will watch while you wire the money to my account and then you can escort me back here.' He wasn't taking her for a fool twice. And he wasn't tak-ing her to bed again, Jules thought bitterly. She had been right about Rand in the first place when she had assumed he was just like her father and Enrique—a manipulative, arrogant, chauvinistic pig.

'But I don't recall sexual favours as being part of our deal, so if you so much as touch me I'm out of here,' she concluded bluntly.

For the second time in less than twenty-four hours the same damn woman rendered Rand Carducci speechless—not a state he enjoyed...

# CHAPTER SEVEN

STANDING under the ice-cold jets of the power shower Rand cursed under his breath. Never in his life had he allowed sex to cloud his judgment so completely and it had to stop. So what if Jules was a sexual innocent? In every other respect she was a hard-hearted bitch and he would do well to remember that. She had walked out on her father and on her fiancé, and indirectly because of Jules' disastrous effect on Enrique Rand had lost his fiancée, Maria, her life cut short in the most brutal way through no fault of her own.

A deep frown marred his dark face; if he was honest he was not exactly innocent of any blame in respect of Maria. He had not seen her for three months at the time of her death, and the only reason she had been at the ranch was because he had said he would meet her there and cancelled at the last minute. Which was probably why she had accepted a ride back to town with Enrique, a ride to her death.

He turned off the shower, stepped out and, picking up a towel, wrapped it around his hips. He was not proud of the way he had treated Maria. He had been young and in the process of setting up his South American network when he had met Maria and fallen in not so much love as lust. They had enjoyed a great night of sex together, and their engagement had been a spur-of-the-moment thing. The only reason it had lasted for years was perhaps because of the proximity of the Diez and Eiga ranches and their mutual ties to the small community. But mostly because Rand had found it convenient and so had Maria while pursuing her singing career. She had never complained about his infrequent visits. But suddenly, after Enrique's engagement had failed, Maria had started pressing Rand for a wedding date, which was why he had postponed his trip the last time. He'd known she would make an amiable wife but he had not been ready to make the decision.

He had loved her in a way. But in fact Jules, with a single glance from her incredible green eyes, could turn him on faster than Maria ever had. With that unsettling thought in his mind, he quickly dressed and left his room.

Jules glanced up as Rand joined her in the back seat of the car, and the grim expression on his harshly handsome face, the deep furrow between his elegantly arched brows, told her all she needed to know. He was back to the cold, aloof man she recalled from her youth, and she was glad, she told herself fiercely. Last night had been a huge mistake and best forgotten. She watched him lean forward and speak to the driver, saw the pull of the grey silk suit across his wide shoulders, and, with a dismaying flicker in the pit of her stomach, she quickly looked away.

The journey was a repeat of the one before. Rand got out his briefcase and buried his head in work; the only difference this time was when Jules happened to glance at his hands she remembered exactly what they could do to her… Their arrival back in the city could not come quick enough for her.

'My bank.' Rand cast her a cold glance as the chauffeur opened the door. 'The money you want will be yours in minutes.'

'Good,' Jules snapped back and slid out of the car. She thanked the driver and followed Rand's broad back up a short flight of stone stairs that led to the massive oak door of the bank. He stopped and she nearly walked into him.

'After you, Jules,' Rand drawled with exaggerated courtesy as he stepped to one side and allowed her to precede him into the hallowed interior of the prestigious private bank in the heart of Santiago.

She did not deign to respond, but simply brushed past him shooting him a vitriolic glance. Five minutes later, seated in a lavishly furnished office, the money having been transferred, she watched the manager of the bank fawning over Rand. Another sycophantic employee served coffee and Jules felt her temperature rising as Rand told the manager they would wait for a telephone confirmation from the English bank that the money was actually in Miss Julia Diez's account.

'Is that all right with you, Jules, darling?' Rand leant towards her and took her hand in his. 'I want you to be in no doubt that I have paid you what you asked.'

Rand was beginning to enjoy himself. He knew the bank manager was amazed that he was making such a procedure out of what to a man of his wealth was a trifling amount of money, and he also knew the manager had drawn entirely the wrong conclusion. Or perhaps not so wrong at that, he had to amend as he realised his thumb was involuntarily stroking the silken skin of her hand. He let go of her hand abruptly, and smiled wryly, slightly ashamed at where his thoughts were leading.

Jules just knew he was trying to make her look like a money-grabbing tart, or, worse, his latest mistress. She could feel the colour rising in her face, but she refused to be intimidated. So what if she came across like that to some bank manager she would never see again in this life? she thought mutinously. She didn't give a damn...because by this time next week her mother would have started her new therapy, and Jules would be able to pay for it, without the worry of bankrupting her business at the same time. But, slanting Rand a glance, she saw his smile and her frustration bubbled over. Two could play at that game, she thought furiously.

'Yes, perfectly,' she responded with a simpering smile of her own that did not reach her eyes. 'But you can't blame a girl for being careful—after all, you did renege on our agreement the first time...' her sparkling green eyes clashed with his '...*Randy, love*,' she drawled huskily and let her hand drop to his thigh and squeezed hard. She felt his muscles tense and his hissed intake of breath, and she nearly cracked up in gales of laughter at the expression of total shock on his dark saturnine features.

*Dio*, but she was a bitch, but she was also full of surprises and a reluctant gleam of amusement illuminated Rand's dark eyes as they challenged hers. 'After the wonder of last night, a mistake I will never repeat, *mia amore*,' he drawled huskily, and covered her hand on his thigh with his own.

Lucky for Jules at that moment the confirmation arrived, and she leapt hastily to her feet.

Five minutes later Jules stood on the pavement, the chauffeur holding open the car door waiting for her to get into the car. She took a step back and cast Rand a cool glance.

'I can walk to my hotel from here, and I'm sure you have much more important things to do than watch me pack, so shall we say an hour or two or three?' she drawled sarcastically.

'I am far too much of a gentleman to contemplate deserting you in a big city, even for a minute. You could get lost,' he shot back silkily, and bundled her into the car.

She wished Rand would *get lost*, Jules thought furiously. She knew exactly what he meant; he did not trust her out of his sight.

It got no better at the hotel. Rand insisted on accompanying her to her room. He helped himself to a bottle of wine from the mini bar, and lounged back against the headboard of the bed while she hurried around repacking her clothes. By the time she was finished Jules was simmering with anger and resentment and something much more primitive... A traitorous desire to join him on the bed.

'If you don't mind I will call my mother before we leave, and tell her I am taking back one of my father's trophies?' She arched a delicate brow enquiringly. 'Unless you have any objection.'

'Be my guest, tell her she can have the lot, if you like. I am in no hurry,' he drawled lazily. 'Are you sure you would not like to join me…?'

The sexual tension in the air was suddenly palpable. Jules shot him a panicked glance. He was lounging back all long-legged, virile male, and she was vividly reminded of another bed. Tearing her gaze away, she picked up the telephone.

'In a glass of wine, of course,' he said with a chuckle that made her even madder.

Trying to ignore him, she swiftly dialled for an outside line and called the familiar number. It would be late afternoon at home and her mother should be in. The sound of her mother's voice brought a lump to her throat. Jules turned her back on Rand and softly enquired about her mother's health, before adding she was fine, enjoying her holiday and she had been right about the ornament. Carlos Diez had left her a trophy from his polo-playing days. Jules heard the catch in her mother's voice.

'I might have guessed—Carlos spent the best part of his life playing polo and spent every cent he had on horses and the ladies. I'm not surprised he left you a trophy. He was obviously still running true to form to the very end, totally blind to anything else in life.'

'You're right there, Mother,' Jules responded and quickly said her goodbyes. There was no sense in telling her mother the truth; it would only upset her.

'You didn't tell your mother about the money,' Rand grated, coming up behind her. 'Why not?'

'I'll tell her when I get home.' The warmth of his breath made the hair on the back of her neck prickle, and, grabbing her suitcase, she turned and thrust past him.

'Because you mean to pocket it all yourself.'

'Humph,' Jules snorted and walked out of the door with a shake of her head. Rand really had the hardest, most cynical mind of anyone she had ever met. Which was probably why he was stinking rich. She doubted many people got rich by being nice, more by being ruthless, she thought reflectively. Look at her own behaviour, her mother would be horrified if she knew she had asked Rand outright for money.

It was a subdued Jules who sat in the back of the car on the return journey to the hacienda, and her mood did not lift over a late buffet lunch provided by Donna on the shaded veranda off the main salon.

The heat from the afternoon sun was ferocious, but if ever a man was given the cold shoulder it was Rand. He had tried to talk to Jules in the car and while they ate, but she had answered in monosyllables if at all. Permafrost had nothing on Jules in this mood, and he did not understand her problem.

She had the money. True, he could have been a bit more gallant about the proceedings, but she had given as good as she'd got. As for the rest, he knew without conceit there wasn't a woman of his acquaintance that would not jump at the chance of spending a few days' holiday in his company. He watched her broodingly as she got to her feet and, with a glance in his direction but without actually making eye contact, she told him she was going to her room for a siesta. It was the last straw for Rand.

'Not so fast,' he bit out harshly, and leapt to his feet. 'If your behaviour in the last few hours is your idea of keeping to our deal and establishing friendly relations between us, then I beg to differ.'

Jules stopped and turned startled green eyes up to his. She hadn't expected such an outburst, but one look into his darkly attractive face and she saw he was fuming. Why was he so angry? She was still here; he had got what he wanted.

'Excuse me, but I don't remember it was ever suggested in our agreement that I had to entertain you every hour of the day. You might be used to women fawning all over you, but not this one... I am here, I am staying the week, and to be honest right about now I don't like you or myself much for that matter.' Jules compressed her lips. 'So the friends thing will have to wait.'

'But I don't want to wait, and after last night ''friends'' is a feeble word for what there is between you and I.'

His provocative statement and the heat in his eyes broke her pensive mood, and Jules went scarlet but managed a slight shrug. 'What there was...' she said sweetly. 'I have no intention of repeating the experience; on reflection—' she paused '—it was not that great.' And on that cutting comment she spun on her heel and headed for the house.

She made it to the foot of the stairs before a strong arm encircled her waist and almost lifted her off her feet.

'Let go of me.'

'I will when we get to your room. On *reflection* you were right, a siesta is a good idea.'

'Not with you.' She tried to wriggle from his hold, but he simply whisked her to the top of the stairs tucked under his arm as if she weighed no more than a feather. 'Put me down,' she snapped, beginning to shake with rage and reaction, much of which was due to the warmth of his arm around her waist and the easy strength he displayed in carrying her. 'You oversexed gorilla. Do you honestly think I would fall into bed with you again after last night?'

Rand set her on her feet, but kept his arm around her waist, and looked down into the emerald eyes sparking with anger and contempt. 'Why not? You have nothing to lose now,' he mocked.

Jules saw red. Her hand flashed through the air and landed with a resounding slap on his lean cheek. 'You bastard.' And she was off along the hall to her room, while he was frozen in shock, his hand to his face.

She dashed into the bedroom, her heart pounding in her chest. She didn't know what had come over her, she was not a violent person, and in fact she had never struck another human being in her life. But Rand Carducci had the ability to bring out the very worst in her.

Suddenly Rand caught up with her, two strong arms entrapping her against his great body.

'You dare to strike me,' he hissed with sibilant softness in her ear, his breath warm against her cheek, and then the heat of his mouth was at her throat. 'I do not take kindly to being assaulted.' His arm crossed over her body, one hand cupping the fullness of her breast, while his other hand slid down over the tautness of her stomach and pressed her closer to the long length of him. 'Know this, Jules—every action has a reaction.'

'Don't you dare,' she warned. The swine's reaction was obvious as the taut muscular angles of his hard body, and more, were pressed against her bottom. She felt his hand tighten on her breast, the pad of his thumb press the tip, and to her shame she felt her nipple peak in instant response. The warm, musky scent of him washed over her, and in a second she was quivering like a leaf in the wind.

She tossed her head from side to side trying to escape the delicious friction of his firm lips against the slender length of her throat, and then his hand pushed down between her thighs. Pinned against him in the most erotic way possible, she was helpless.

'Haven't you realised yet? I dare anything, Jules, and if you were honest you would admit you want it too, have done all day.' Then in one deft movement he turned her in his arms and kissed her.

Immediately Jules was swept up in a maelstrom of passion, the world and everything in it lost in the heady, uncontrollable excitement of his kiss, his arms tight around her, his mouth with devastating hunger plunging her ever further into the deep, dark depths of an ungovernable desire. She clung to him, her heart racing, her pulse pounding, her every nerve and muscle taut with a hunger, a need only Rand could assuage. She felt the moist heat between her thighs and she writhed instinctively against the rock-hard length of him.

He swept her up against his chest and walked across to the bed. She felt the mattress at the back of her knees, and then she tumbled backwards onto the bed, his great body following her down.

'Yes.' One dark brow arched as he stared down at her, his hard-boned features grim and taut. 'Say it, Jules,' he commanded and she did.

They came together in a fierce frenzied coupling, and she was ready for him, more than ready. Her skirt was pushed around her waist, and frantically she tore at his trousers. She cried out as he thrust hard and deep, and then it was all heat and sweat-slicked savage passion, culminating in a wild, explosive climax they reached together.

Jules lay half on the bed and stared dazedly up into his dark, handsome face. He looked almost as shocked as she felt. 'What happened?' she asked bemusedly.

Sudden vibrant amusement lightened the dark passion in Rand's eyes. He reached for her and hauled her up onto the bed and lay half over her. 'Well, if you don't know, perhaps I should show you again,' he rasped throatily. 'But first let's dispense with the rest of these clothes.'

Naked flesh to flesh, he lowered his head to hers, one hand skimming up her back to lift her up as their lips met slowly, tenderly, and to Jules' amazement she trembled, the fire igniting again in her belly.

If she had thought what had gone before was perfect, what followed was paradise. With skill and tenderness Rand kissed and caressed every inch of her body and she returned the favour, glorying in discovering the taste and texture of every bronzed inch of him. When he finally lifted her over him and thrust up into the moist heart of her, she tossed back her head and moaned her delight as he drove her to the edge over and over again. Holding her fast when she would have ridden him to the end, until she thought she would die from the pleasure. Until with a swivel of her hips he lost control, and they rolled across the bed and came in a cataclysmic storm of release.

Jules lay flat on her back and stared up at Rand. He bent his head and pressed a tender kiss on her cheek, her brow, her nose; his hand skimmed up over her breasts to wind into her tumbling hair and sweep it from her face and shoulder.

'After your disparaging remark after lunch, dare I ask was that great, or do I need more practice?' Rand rasped, breathing heavily.

Jules saw the golden glitter of all-male satisfaction in the depths of his dark eyes, and knew he did not really need an answer. Rand was so sure of his virile masculinity, and with good reason.

'You know you don't, and great is a poor adjective for such a mind-blowing experience,' she wryly acknowledged. 'Not that I am any expert,' she tagged on. Rand's ego was big enough without her inflating it any further.

'Maybe not, but you are a remarkably fast and eager learner.' Rand grinned, and dropped a kiss on the tip of her breast.

She felt her nipple tighten and couldn't believe it.

'It must be this place—Chile,' Jules said. 'I never feel like this at home. Yet the first time I came here I fell for Enrique, and this time you. It is uncanny—as if the Latin half of me wakes up when I step off the plane into the heat.' She tried to justify her wild behaviour more to herself than to Rand.

A husky chuckle greeted her comment. 'If I did not know you were a virgin until last night, a lesser man might take offence at that remark, Jules, my sweet. First lesson in post-coital conversation: never mention another man's name,' Rand prompted and collapsed on his back and turned her into the crook of his arm, holding her close. 'Though I am curious why you and Enrique never made love... Knowing Enrique, I am amazed by his patience. After all, you were engaged...did you insist on waiting for the wedding night?'

Jules shifted uncomfortably in the curve of his arm, and then thought after what they had shared she might as well tell him the truth. She wanted Rand. There was no point in trying to deny it any more even though a part of her was afraid of what he could make her feel; she didn't want to fall in love with the man. But continuing their affair held great appeal. However, she was also acutely aware that if they were to have any hope of continuing the relationship there had to be some trust between them, so she might as well start.

'I don't think Enrique ever really wanted me as a lover.' And rolling over onto Rand's chest, she looked candidly up into his black eyes.

'My father lied. I did not break off the wedding because I thought I was too young, or because I wanted fun.' She saw his dark eyes narrow disbelievingly, and she hauled herself up to a sitting position and looked down at him. She felt slightly more in control that way.

'And?' Rand prompted, folding his hands behind his head, his great body apparently relaxed.

'Three days before the wedding I paid Enrique a surprise visit, and found him with another woman.'

'It could have been perfectly innocent,' Rand suggested smoothly. 'I know how impulsive you can be. Did you give him a chance to explain?' His eyes were fixed on her but without any perceptible emotion at all. 'The woman might have just been a friend.'

Either he was a very good liar, or he really did not know about Maria and Enrique. Jules had no idea what had split them up, but Rand must have really loved Maria once and she knew the truth would hurt him, and her soft heart would not let her deliberately cause him pain. Instead she opted for a blasé response.

'Stark naked, rolling around in each other's arms.' She slanted him a wry glance. 'I don't think so, Rand.'

*'Dio mio!'* he exclaimed in disbelief. 'You were little more than a child at the time and you saw them.' He turned onto his side and propped his head on one hand, his attention fully arrested. 'No wonder you ran away. Did you know the woman?'

'No,' she lied and avoided his concerned gaze. 'But when I told my father he said I should forget about it and marry Enrique anyway.'

'Well, I suppose everyone is entitled to one mistake.'

'You are joking!' Jules exclaimed heatedly. 'Infidelity is unforgivable in my book, and if that was not enough,' she added, 'try my father admitting Enrique was only marrying me so the two ranches could be joined together. I am amazed a man of your business acumen had not worked that out for yourself. But then you would probably agree with my father on that score—you men all stick together.'

'No. No, Jules.' Rand jerked up out of his lounging position, and for a second she could have sworn she caught a flicker of guilt in his black eyes before his heavy lids lowered veiling his reaction, and abruptly he pulled her into the warmth of his great body and kissed her.

'Never mistake me for your father, or any other man for that matter, Jules. I would never intentionally hurt you.'

In that moment Jules believed him. It was there in the dark intensity of his gaze and the tender smile on his wonderfully sensuous mouth.

Three days later Jules stretched languorously on the bed, her emerald gaze following Rand's naked body as he walked around her bedroom retrieving his hastily discarded clothes and putting them on.

She smiled a slow, tender curve of her full lips as he pulled on his jeans and glanced across at her.

'Whoever said a siesta was meant for resting from the heat of the day had never met a woman like you.' Rand grinned back. 'And this dodging Donna and Sanchez is no joke.'

'Well, it was your suggestion, oh mighty one!' She gave him a lascivious glance. 'To protect my reputation.'

The past few days had been like a dream for Jules. She had accompanied Rand on long leisurely rides over the ranch, and been reacquainted with the employees. She had spent many a happy hour with the womenfolk and children, while Rand, as was the custom, had discussed business solely with the men. Jules had even picked up one or two recipes she thought would be beneficial to her own business.

But best of all every night in her bed, and most afternoons, they made wild, wanton love before Rand slipped back to his own room, so as not to upset the sensibilities of Donna and her husband. A fleeting shadow dulled Jules' expressive eyes; the idyll must end soon, she knew. Tomorrow afternoon she was booked on a flight back to England.

'There would be no need to protect your reputation,' Rand responded, strolling over to sit down on the side of the bed, his fingers idly toying with a stray curl of hair falling over her slender shoulder. 'If you want to reconsider your options, my offer to marry you still stands.'

For a moment Jules could not breathe. Was he serious? With every day that passed she was finding it harder and harder to keep up the light-hearted repartee with no mention of a future, and she was in real danger of falling hopelessly in love with the man if she let herself. Now for an instant a flicker of hope ignited in her heart and was just as quickly extinguished as he continued.

'For the next three weeks technically, then the codicil is void anyway. But if you want to stay here for a year just say the word.' She stiffened as his head bent and his lips brushed her brow. 'Think about it, Jules. Tomorrow you are scheduled to return home, and I am heading for Japan the day after. I could pull a few strings and we could get married in a civil ceremony before I leave. There is no reason why you should not stop here and I will visit as often as I can and in a year's time you will be much better off.'

'And divorced.' She needed to hear Rand say it, to spell out how little importance he put on marriage, on her…

'Yes, of course,' he agreed briskly, and reached to draw her into his arms, but she rolled across the bed and sat up, her feet finding the floor.

With her back to him she fought to control her breathing, the pain like a knife in her heart. Their brief affair was almost over and she had to accept that and stop hoping for more.

'Thanks, but no, thanks,' she threw over her shoulder and stood up. Rand was not into commitment. It was that simple and she had to be adult about it, tease and joke the same way Rand did so effortlessly.

Slowly she turned around to look down at where he sat on the other side of the bed, for once totally unconscious of her splendid nudity, all her considerable will-power concentrated on making her voice light as she told him, 'I have a life, a business, family and friends in England. A pleasant interlude is one thing, but a semi-permanent arrangement...' She shrugged her slender shoulders and attempted a smile. 'You probably know better than me how futile that would be.'

'Yes, you're right, but I felt honour bound to make the offer before you left.' Rand got to his feet and picked up his shirt from the foot of the bed and slipped it on. 'Forget I mentioned it.'

His words only confirmed what Jules had recognised for herself, and her chin lifted fractionally. 'I already have,' she declared brightly and his glittering dark gaze skimmed over her in a near sensual assault.

'Good, I am glad we are agreed.' He reached for her in one supple movement and pulled her to him. 'But as our time is limited, *cara*...' he drawled suggestively and kissed her.

She could have fought... But Rand was right, their time together was limited. She had a lifetime for regret...but only one night left for love...

# CHAPTER EIGHT

A LONG sensual interlude later Rand was once again pulling on his clothes. 'I have never dressed as many times in a day in my life as I have since I met you.' He grinned at Jules, sticking his crumpled shirt into the waistband of his jeans. 'But you are worth it.'

Jules tightened the belt of her cotton wrap, and with the width of the bed between them grinned back. 'So are you.' Not the most brilliant repartee, but she found it impossible to stay hurt or angry with Rand when he made love to her. She had to take him for what he was and enjoy the moment, she told herself fatalistically.

His low, husky chuckle feathered her nerve endings and she stood rooted to the spot as he approached her and caught her arm in a light clasp. 'A compliment from you, Jules—a first. Shame I don't have the time to show my appreciation.' It was impossible to still the faint trembling of her body and yet she drew comfort from the touch of his hand. 'But I have some business I must attend to.' He dropped a light kiss on the tip of her nose. 'I'll see you later, *cara*.' And left.

Jules strolled out of the kitchen, an apple in her hand plus a couple of sugar lumps, and headed for the stable block, her pensive gaze sweeping over the landscape.

Tomorrow she was leaving all this behind, and her common sense told her she would never return. Her life was not in South America, never had been, but she could not help the bittersweet memories flickering through her mind.

She pushed open the stable door and walked inside. Six stalls lined one side and the other side was tack rooms and an office. Polly whinnied at her approach, and Jules' lips parted in the briefest of smiles. 'It's all right, girl.' She reached the stall and stroked Polly's nose. 'A special treat, two sugar lumps and an apple.' And, stroking the gentle animal, she gave her the food.

She had no idea how long she stayed, hugging and stroking the beautiful mare, but, finally blinking back the tears, she murmured,

'Goodbye, Polly,' and, head bent, she walked away.

The sound of a car screeching to a halt broke through her haze of sadness, and, looking up, she realised she had walked around the side of the hacienda and an open-topped Mercedes had drawn up at the front door.

One glance at the occupants and she instinctively took a hasty step back. Señor Eiga was the driver, and Rand the passenger. She had not actually got around the corner so they could not have seen her, she told herself, her heart racing.

She was about to slip away when she heard Rand's deep, dark voice.

'Are you sure I can't persuade you to come to dinner?'

Oh, my God, no! Jules' face froze and she stood paralysed with shock. Señor Eiga was her idea of the dinner guest from hell, especially as it was her last night here. But what followed was even worse.

'No, definitely not. I tell you, Randolfo, you must have the patience of a saint to put up with that evil woman for a day, never mind a week.

If I saw her I don't think I could keep my hands off her after what she did to my son.'

'Fine by me. Dismiss her from your mind, Señor Eiga. I can assure you everything is taken care of. Julia Diez is leaving here tomorrow, and you will never see her again. As for the ranch, I will meet you and your lawyer tomorrow morning as arranged and sign the necessary sale documents, with the one proviso as we agreed.'

'Seven years but at last the two properties amalgamated as they were meant to be. I have you to thank, Randolfo, and, given the depth of your own loss, I have to congratulate you on your remarkable performance. It could not have been easy for you, sweet-talking that woman into letting you do what we wanted. Carlos, for all his delusion at the end that caused so much delay, I think would be proud of you. God rest his soul.'

Jules heard the car drive away, and the sound of the front door being opened and closed, and weakly she sank back against the wall. She could not believe what she had heard, didn't want to.

Tilting her head back, she took great gulps of the sweet-scented night air. The first star twinkled to life in the swiftly darkening sky, but she felt as if the light of her life had just gone out. She wanted to scream her anguish to the heavens... She had been played for a fool all over again.

The codicil to her father's will, stating she must marry Rand to inherit anything. It had all been a big game to Rand; he had never intended going through with it. He must have been delighted when as executor he had called to inform her of the codicil and she had said she was not interested, and then horrified when she had turned up in the last month.

It would be funny if it were not so devious of him. Obviously with his stepmother Ester's approval he had already arranged to sell the property to Señor Eiga. Rand's insistence that Jules sign an option for him to buy her share of the property whether she married him or not, she had thought odd at the time, an option on a mythical inheritance and signed without a qualm, but now it made perfect sense. That was all he had really wanted. Like the ruthless businessman he was, he had covered all the bases. He had insisted she stay the week, and if she changed her mind about marriage he was happy to comply, sure in the knowledge that, if she did, he could sell the ranch at the end of the year. Presenting himself as oh, so honourable! When all he'd wanted was her signature on the document.

He had even let her humiliate herself and ask for what to him was a paltry amount of money. He must have been howling with laughter behind her back. He probably thought it was a huge joke to make love to her as well, an added bonus... While Jules had hoped for more...

Three days ago in bed with Rand she had nurtured the secret wish that their relationship might continue when they left here. She had confided in him the truth of her broken engagement, thinking it would build trust between them. What kind of naive idiot did that make her?

No... She would not be a victim, not for any man, and especially not for Rand Carducci. Slowly she straightened up and glanced around, her heart a lead weight in her chest. Nothing had changed here in years, and nothing ever would, she realised bitterly. Every man she had ever met in this place was a pure male chauvinist pig. Her mother had been right when she'd said it was best to cut every single tie with the Diez family and friends.

Jules' one consolation in the whole devastating affair was that at least she had turned Rand down when he had suggested the marriage of convenience. Not once, but twice. If she had accepted that would have been a humiliation too much to bear. As it was she did not know how she was going to face the man without scratching his eyes out. But she had to; her pride demanded no less.

'Where have you been?' Donna demanded a few moments later as Jules walked into the kitchen. 'Señor Randolfo has been looking for you.'

'Saying goodbye to Polly.' It was true and also explained away the sadness she could not quite disguise. 'And I'll see Rand at dinner anyway.'

'Yes, well—' Donna smiled '—don't worry, Polly will be well looked after, and you better hurry and dress. Dinner will be served in thirty minutes.'

Armour was what she needed, and half an hour later, when Jules walked into the dining room, armour was exactly what she had got. She had utilised every lesson she had ever learned about make-up. Her huge eyes were accentuated with the skilful use of eyeliner and mascara, her lip-gloss coated and coated again with a sheen like glass. Her long auburn hair was brushed into a silken screen to fall in soft curls down her back, a few strands artfully curled in apparent disarray around the perfect oval of her face.

Tiny shoestring straps supported a simple black crêpe dress that revealed the creamy mounds of her breasts, and was cut on the bias to cling lovingly to her narrow waist and softly flaring hips, and end mid-thigh.

Jules had bought it and never worn it, afraid it was too short and too revealing. She had stuck it into her suitcase at the last minute thinking it might be okay in a hot climate.

'Jules.' Rand stopped, the glass of whisky in his hand suspended halfway to his mouth when he caught sight of her.

'Donna said you were looking for me.' She walked towards him on slender-heeled black sandals. 'Nothing important, I hope?' she prompted, barely able to conceal the cynicism in her tone. Maybe he was not a complete bastard and was going to tell her about Señor Eiga buying the ranch, but she wouldn't bet on it! And the devious devil did not disappoint…

'No.' He shook his head as she stopped in front of him.

The arrested expression on his harshly attractive face might have made her laugh at any other time. But her armour was not just on the outside. Inside her emotions had curdled into a rock-hard lump of icy fury that not even the staggering effect of his powerful body clad in a tailored white dinner jacket and dark trousers could melt.

She smiled. 'Are you going to pour me a drink, or what?'

'I'd take the ''or what'' in a flash, except Donna is going to serve the meal any minute,' Rand teased huskily. 'You look exquisite, Jules. I hardly dare kiss you.'

'Then don't… At least not until after dinner.' She glanced up at him through the thick fringe of her lashes, saw his head begin to lower, and added, 'I can hear Donna now, and I'm starving.'

She sat down in the chair Rand pulled out for her, and smiled when he took the seat at the head of the table. She smiled again when he filled her glass with the finest vintage champagne. Jules kept on smiling through one delicious course after another, though if asked she could not have said what she ate.

They conversed on a variety of subjects from the European common market to the relative merits of living in a cold climate as opposed to a temperate one like Italy. But Jules was no longer fooled by his sophisticated charm and was constantly aware of the passion under the surface of the light, sometimes flirtatious conversation. It was there in the hooded dark eyes that followed her every move…it was lust…brutal and basic…

Jules gave him another chance to tell her the truth later in the salon. 'So what will happen to the Diez Ranch now?' she asked as Donna left the room after delivering the coffee. She leant forward and filled two cups and, turning slightly, she handed one to Rand sitting on the sofa beside her.

'Nothing. Donna and Sanchez and hopefully a little Sanchez will carry on as before.' Rand grinned and took the cup from her hand, and drained it in one go, before putting it back on the table.

Jules had all the confirmation she wanted; Rand was a deceitful, lying swine. She shook her head in disgust.

'Don't worry your head about it, Jules,' Rand murmured, totally misreading her reaction, and, lifting a hand, he trailed it down her cheek. He traced the curve of her mouth with a gentle forefinger. 'You look so incredibly beautiful I am almost afraid to touch you.' Then he lowered his head and placed a fleeting kiss on her mouth. 'I've wanted to do that all evening and more,' he said slightly unsteadily, drawing back.

Jules' lashes drifted down over her eyes; she did not want to see the lies in his eyes, but she was going to have this one last night. 'Me too,' she murmured and slid her hand into his, and slowly rose to her feet. 'Shall we go up?' she asked boldly.

Slightly surprised at her forwardness, Rand sucked in a breath and stood up. 'Lead on,' he bit out, his fingers flexing around hers as he allowed her to lead him from the room.

His dark gaze roamed over the glorious mass of red hair falling down her back and fixed on the erotic sway of her *derrière* as they mounted the stairs, tension riding him. It was a fantasy come true to be led to bed by the exquisite Jules, and he determined to see just how far her sexual bravery extended. Five minutes later it took every ounce of his self-control not to grab her and throw her on the bed as she subjected him to a slow striptease. Tease being the operative word.

Jules stopped by the side of the bed and let go of his hand and turned around to face him. She saw the barely controlled need in the depths of his night-black eyes, the slight anticipatory smile curving his sensuous mouth, *like a lamb to the slaughter,* she thought bitterly. But as slaughter was not an option for the conniving fiend unless she wanted to spend her life in a Chilean jail, she was determined to make this a night he would never forget.

'Our last night,' she murmured throatily and, reaching up, slipped his jacket from his shoulders, allowing her hands to sweep up and cup his head and bring it down to hers. She bit on his bottom lip and then briefly flicked her tongue into the welcoming heat of his mouth, before withdrawing quickly.

'No. We need to undress first,' she commanded as he would have deepened the kiss, and, sliding her fingers under the fine straps of her dress, she slipped first one and then the other down her arms and off.

With the bodice slipping down around her waist, her breasts exposed to his avid view, she lifted her hands and flicked them through the long mass of hair, throwing her head back.

Teasingly she licked the tip of her tongue over her lips. 'I can taste you, Rand.' She let her hands drop to cup her breasts, and slowly ran her thumbs over the tips. 'And I have been aching all night,' she confided huskily, gently massaging the perfect creamy globes before dipping her hands lower and, with a slow, deliberate shimmy of her hips, allowed the dress to fall in a pool of fabric at her feet.

She glanced up at him through the thick fringe of her lashes, and saw he had got rid of his shirt and his trousers, but the arrested expression on his rugged face was all she could have hoped for. She noted the heavy rise and fall of his chest, and hid a smile, before stepping forward and suggestively rubbing her breasts against his naked chest.

'Jules, you temptress.' Rand groaned through obviously gritted teeth. 'What are you trying to do to me?'

She curved her hands around his hips. 'What would you like me to do to you?' she asked throatily, and before he could form a reply she sank down to her knees and took his shorts with her. 'Something like this?'

She heard his harshly indrawn breath, and boldly took the evidence of his desire in her hands. One part of her was amazed at her daring and sizzling with excitement while another part of her was coldly determined to do everything she could think of to bring the arrogant devil to his knees.

Her tongue flicked the velvet tip, and her lips caressed him. His hands raked through her hair and she heard him moan. She tilted her head back and glanced up at him; his eyes were closed and a dark tide of colour suffused his high cheekbones, his firm lips pulled tight with tension.

'You like that?' she murmured and touched him again.

'*Dio!*' He suddenly hauled her up hard against him, and his mouth captured hers in a savage open-mouthed kiss, even as he tumbled her back on the bed.

'Torment me, would you?' Rand grated. 'Let me return the favour.' And, pinning her hands above her head, he stretched full length on top of her, then proceeded to kiss and caress down her body. He sucked the aching peaks of her breasts one by one, then lightly bit the hard nipples, creating an exquisite torture that made her moan with pleasure. He released her hands and she grasped his wide shoulders as his head dipped lower and circled her navel with his tongue and then lower still.

She writhed wildly beneath him, but his strong hands held her thighs as his mouth wreaked devastation on her most vulnerable spot. A strangled moan of feverish ecstasy escaped her, and she had no thought in her head but the agonising desire for release. Rand stilled, and looked up, his black eyes smouldering as her body shuddered and her pelvis lifted instinctively. The fingers of one hand scratched down his back and with the other she reached for his rock-hard erection and closed over the straining flesh.

Rand made an animalistic groan and reared back, dislodging her hand, and hauled her over his thighs and thrust deep and huge inside her. It was fast and furious, their bodies locked in a fierce, primeval rhythm, and Jules clung to him as his powerful life force filled her shaking, shuddering body.

A long time later as the aftershock of their ferocious mating faded Rand gently withdrew and eased her back against the pillows. 'Jules, *cara*,' he murmured, and gently stroked her hair back from her face. 'You never cease to surprise me.' His dark eyes looked lazily down into hers. 'I don't know what I will do without you. You're incredible'

Jules had a pretty damn good idea, she thought bitterly, her heart hardening as she listened to his softly mouthed platitudes. He was so smooth, so sophisticated and she had to have been mad to ever get involved with him. His naked body gleamed dark golden and sweat slicked in the dim light of the bedside lamp and helplessly she acknowledged he was also a demon lover. But she had not the least doubt some willing woman would be waiting for him in Japan or back home in Italy. What kind of idiot did he take her for? Rand lied as he did everything else…to perfection.

'So are you.' She whispered the lie back to him, and, closing her eyes, she let her hands roam over the perfection of his body yet again. It would be time enough tomorrow to tell him what she really thought of him, and she gave herself up to the pleasures of the flesh.

Anger and resentment simmered through Jules as Rand rolled over onto his side and within seconds the even sound of his breathing told her he was fast asleep. But sleep was a long time coming for Jules; she lay wide awake and studied the man at her side. They had made love over and over again and she had long since given up on trying to decide who was seducing whom. The first rays of dawn illuminated his sleeping figure, and a bitter smile twisted her love-swollen lips. She might not have scratched his eyes out, but she had done a jolly good job on the satin-smooth skin of his broad back. Serves him right, she thought, but it was small consolation for the way he had deceived her, and finally she fell into a restless sleep.

When she opened her eyes again she was alone in the bed, and a washed and dressed Rand was depositing a coffee tray on the bedside table.

He straightened up and smiled down at her and the intimate gleam in his dark eyes set off an involuntary wave of excitement through her veins. She stifled a groan. No man had a right to look so good; the pale grey suit he was wearing accentuated the physical perfection of his magnificent body and the white shirt contrasted sexily with his tanned skin, a skin she had known every inch of! Her nipples went hard with the thought of what they had done to each other last night in this very bed, and she could do nothing about her suddenly pink cheeks.

'Good morning.' Rand surveyed her with a blatant masculine appreciation. 'You looked as though you needed your rest when I left you.' He bent down and pressed a swift kiss on the top of her head. 'And I convinced Donna she needed a rest from the stairs and to concentrate on breakfast while I delivered the coffee.'

More colour heated her skin but she managed a polite, 'Thank you.'

'I would let you thank me properly, but time is running out.' He caught her eyes and gave her a surprisingly tender smile. 'Unless you have changed your mind about marrying me, Jules.'

She could not believe the audacity of the man. He was so damn sure he was home free, and for a second she was tempted to give the conceited devil the shock of his life and say yes. That would knock the lying smile off his face.

'No way,' she said quickly, and tore her gaze away from his before she could give in to the impulsive idea. 'I will be packed and ready to leave in twenty minutes, and tell Donna just toast will do for me.'

'There is no great hurry. I do have a bit of business to attend to this morning, before we leave.'

Jules knew just what kind, and it only served to incense her further.

'Hey, don't worry about me, take your time. I am perfectly capable of making my own way to the airport.'

'Are you okay, Jules?' He frowned down at her, something in his tone telling her he had picked up on her less than enthusiastic response.

'Yes, fine,' she replied crisply. 'But I do have to get a move on. I have to pack.'

'Yes, I know.' Rand straightened to his full height, but she caught the flicker of puzzlement in his eyes before he turned and left.

Two hours later Jules followed Rand out to the waiting car. She had paid a visit to Polly with a sugar lump and said a tearful goodbye to Donna, and been frigidly polite to Rand when he had appeared in the kitchen just twenty minutes ago.

She knew where he had been, not a mile away with Señor Eiga and his lawyers. It took all her considerable self-control to look him in the eye, and she knew he sensed something was wrong, but he was too much of a gentleman to cause a scene in front of Donna. But Jules was not too much of a lady to cause a scene once she got in the car. She was going to tell Rand exactly what she thought of him, and then some…

Unfortunately Jules was too much of a lady to cause a scene in front of Sanchez, and for some reason he had taken over from the chauffeur and was driving them to Santiago.

'Why is Sanchez driving?' she demanded of Rand as soon as he joined her in the back seat.

He looked surprised. 'Does it matter?' he drawled.

His sardonic tone annoyed her and hostile green eyes flashed to his. 'No. No, of course not.'

'Then why the glare?'

'Do you have to be so sarcastic?'

His dark brows lifted. 'If I sounded sarcastic, I can assure you I did not intend it that way. As it happens, Sanchez has some business to attend to in Santiago, and what is your English saying? To kill two birds with one stone. Somehow, for a nation that prides itself on being animal lovers, I find the sentiment rather brutal.' He gave her a slow, charmingly intimate smile. Jules wished she were impervious to it, but she wasn't; her body's response was immediate, and shaming.

'I suppose so,' she murmured, turning away to look out of the window and hide the heat in her face, the sudden pulsing in her neck. Angry as she was, she realised confrontation in the car was out; she did not want to offend Sanchez. Lost in her own thoughts, she feigned sleep for the rest of the journey.

She thought of her mother, and realised very soon she would be home, and with the realisation came another: Liz had not wanted her to accept anything from her father's estate. Yet Jules had the money she needed to make her mother better. Did it really matter that Rand had been devious about the sale of the ranch? Basically he had paid her off so he could clinch a deal on the sale of the ranch quickly. She supposed in a way he had done her a favour. Jules had the money, and, being brutally honest, her late father would not even have given her that.

All she really wanted she had got, and all she really wanted to do now was get back home among her friends and never return to Chile as long as she lived. As for Rand, he was a devious devil, and she would be much better off trying to forget about the love affair or, to be more precise, the lust affair as of now. She would never see him again after today so there was no point in confronting him, and with her mind made up she did fall asleep.

But a few hours later, standing in the VIP departure lounge at the airport, she changed her mind. Rand, true to his word, had escorted her to the airport, and now with an arm around her shoulder he turned her to face him.

'I know what is bothering you, Jules—you have been like a cat on a hot tin roof all morning.' He studied her from beneath thick black lashes. 'And I know the emotional intensity of the past week must have been a shock for you.' He lifted a hand to caress her cheek. 'But, believe me, everything will be fine.' And then he smiled, a brilliant smile of unconcealed triumph, and like a magician pulling a rabbit from a hat he added, 'As soon as I return from Japan I will call you and we can take up from where we left off.'

Outraged by the sheer *bloody* confidence of the man, Jules felt the fragile control she had held on her temper since last night finally break under the strain. 'You can call until you are blue in the face, but I sure as hell won't answer.' She felt his arm tighten around her

waist and she flattened her hands on his chest
to prevent him drawing her any closer.

'What is the matter with you?' Rand demanded forcefully, the hand caressing her
cheek curving under her chin, his narrow-eyed
gaze intent on her furious face.

'Nothing, now I am leaving you,' she
snapped. 'You lying swine, do you think I
don't know why you wanted the sale option on
my mythical half of the ranch? Do you think
I don't know you had already done a deal to
sell the ranch to Señor Eiga? What kind of
idiot do you take me for?'

He stiffened, a ridge of colour etching his
high cheekbones, and his hand fell from her
face and she was free. 'I did not take you for
an idiot. I took you because I wanted you,' he
drawled mockingly. 'As for the rest...it was
business.' He surveyed her with dark, cynical
eyes. 'You should understand that—after all,
you only came here for money. But enlighten
me, Jules—who told you about the so-called
deal?'

'You and Señor Eiga,' she flared back at
him. 'So there is no point denying it.'

Rand's cold eyes raked her pale, set face. 'I wouldn't dream of it,' he said harshly. 'But it is good to know what you really think of me before I wasted any more of my time.'

For the space of a heartbeat Jules thought she saw a flash of something—disappointment?—pass over his face—or pain perhaps? But she was quickly disabused of the notion when he gestured with a long-fingered hand to the departure board. 'They have called your flight, and I would hate for you to miss it, Jules.'

Instinctively she turned her head to read the board, and sure enough the flight to London Heathrow was now listed as boarding. She turned back in time to see Rand, head and shoulders above everyone else, heading for the exit. He hadn't bothered to say goodbye!

# CHAPTER NINE

'For heaven's sake, Jules, stop fussing!' Tina exclaimed. 'Everything is ready, but if we don't start serving in the next five minutes we will be in trouble.'

'I know.' Jules grinned at her friend. 'But this is one of the best contracts we have ever had. If Sir Peter Hatton is pleased with our firm, and passes the word around to his wealthy friends, it will be a great boost to our contract catering.'

'True. But let's just concentrate on this dinner first.'

Jules placed the starters on two trays—smoked salmon with avocado and walnut salad—and then with an anxious glance at her mother she asked, 'Are you sure you don't mind serving, Mum?'

'No, not at all, my six-month check was clear and with my new treatment I feel great, so stop worrying. It is not your fault that your two casual girls are on a school ski trip this week, and this is too good a deal to turn down.'

'Okay.' Jules waved a hand. 'Then get moving with that tray.'

They were catering a private dinner party for twelve in the large manor house of Sir Peter Hatton. Iris had taken the booking, and it was their most prestigious to date. Iris was her mother's lifelong friend, who had worked for her since Liz had first bought the business when her father had died and Jules was only two. Now Iris' daughter Tina and her husband John also worked for the firm, and it was Iris who had run the bakery and kept an eye on her mother when Jules had been in Chile.

Seated at the magnificent dining table, Rand could hardly contain his impatience to get the meal over and done with. He had caught a glimpse of two vehicles as he'd arrived at the hall emblazoned with 'Jules Corporate Catering' and beneath 'A Gem of a Service'—a play on words that had brought a brief smile to his face for the first time in two months.

Peter Hatton was a business acquaintance of Rand's who happened to own a large estate a few miles away from Jules' home town. Rand had offered to do a deal with him over a trout farm Peter had been trying to sell for ages, on condition he held a celebratory dinner party at his home, at Rand's expense, of course, and he would arrange the catering. Though what Rand was going to do with a trout farm he had no idea! But it meant he would see Jules again.

Ester had been satisfied at the way the Diez estate had finally been settled but she was worried that he had still not told Jules the whole truth, and could not understand the delay, as he and the girl were friends!

He hadn't the heart to tell her Jules would probably shoot him as soon as look at him, after the way they had parted the last time.

Usually Rand was in favour of the direct approach where women were concerned, but with Jules it was different. She had got under his skin like no woman before, and, estate business aside, he ached to see her for himself. But he knew if he called at her home she would slam the door in his face, which was not a scenario he relished. If he was honest he was scared at the thought of seeing her again because he was even more afraid that after

talking to him she might never want to see him
again.

Rand Carducci frightened of a woman was
a first, but he did not think his pride could take
another rejection, hence the elaborate charade.

A chance meeting, an explanation, and if
she accepted the truth, and if he sensed she
was amiable to renewing their affair, he would
take it from there. He told himself he was being circumspect because he was still not totally
convinced she was the *gem* of a woman she
appeared. Great sex, the best he had ever had,
did not necessarily mean she had a great character to match.

Social nicety decreed Rand respond politely
to the conversational gambits of the ladies
seated either side of him—one was Hatton's
cousin Pat—but his eyes kept straying to the
dining-room door, and when it finally opened
and two waitresses appeared a cursory glance
told him Jules obviously didn't serve the food.

'My goodness! It is you, Liz.'

Rand glanced to his right and saw Pat was
addressing the older of the two waitresses as
she placed the starter in front of her. 'I didn't

know you worked as a waitress—I thought you ran a bakery in the town.'

His attention arrested, Rand looked harder at the waitress—mid forties, he guessed, and quite beautiful with pale blonde hair. His dark eyes widened in shock as he realised the green eyes were unmistakable—it had to be Jules' mother. Quite deliberately, he tuned into their conversation, then, utilising all his considerable charm, he subtly questioned Pat.

Flattered by his undivided attention, the lady gossiped quite freely, telling Rand the intimate details about her breast cancer and the fact she had met Liz, who had the same problem, on the day they had both attended a private clinic to begin a new expensive treatment. Pat ended by confiding that Liz had told her she had no private medical care, so she could only surmise Liz's bakery must be a little gold-mine for her to be able to afford the treatment, and mentioned the cost of the three-year course.

The price quoted made Rand pale beneath his tan. He had heard that figure before, and suddenly the reason for Jules' demand for money was glaringly obvious. He spent the rest of the meal cursing himself for a blind fool under his breath, the food almost choking him.

With the kitchen to herself for a moment Jules reflected on her good fortune and realised at last life was looking up for her and her mum. Liz was making a remarkable recovery from her breast cancer, and Jules was slowly getting over her disastrous love affair. Rand still haunted her dreams but she had progressed from thinking about him every minute of the day when she'd first returned home, to going almost a whole day without thinking about him at all. Plus she had the satisfaction of knowing her heartache had been worth it just to see the rapid improvement in her mother's health.

Holding that thought, Jules concentrated on the final preparation of the main course. Roast stuffed saddle of lamb, garnished renaissance-style with artichoke bottoms filled with carrot and turnips. French beans, peas, asparagus tips, cauliflower coated with hollandaise sauce and new potatoes. Very suitable for a spring evening at the end of March.

'Jules, you will never guess who is here,' Liz declared. 'You remember me telling you I met Pat Jenson the first time I went to the private clinic and she was a patient too? Well, she is one of the dinner guests, and she is the cousin of Sir Peter Hatton. I have had coffee with her several times and she never mentioned it.'

'Very nice, Mum,' Jules said, not paying much attention, too involved in her cooking, and for the next few hours little was said as all three worked hectically to present the meal.

'That is it,' Tina declared after returning from serving the coffee with Liz. 'I am whacked.'

Jules glanced around the kitchen. She had cleared up as she'd gone along, and John had almost finished loading the van. Apart from collecting the coffee-cups there was nothing more to do, so she told her mum and Tina to go home.

'I'll wait for the dregs and present the bill, and follow you later.' Experience had taught her coffee stage could last anything from half an hour to three, and there was no point in them all hanging around. John collected the last of the equipment, and all three left with a cheery goodnight.

Jules withdrew the already prepared invoice from her document case and placed it on the bench, then swiftly stripped off her white chef's jacket and hat, and sighed with relief.

It was true what they said about heat in the kitchen; she was wet with sweat. Smoothing a few damp tendrils of hair away from her brow, she pulled off the ribbon holding her hair back, and shook her head, then eased her white tee shirt free from her checked cotton chef's trousers. Crossing to the coffee-maker, she filled a cup and sat down at the kitchen table to wait. All in all, she thought it had been a very successful evening, and hopefully Sir Peter Hatton would recommend the firm to his friends.

Leaning back in the chair, she sighed contentedly and, lifting her coffee-cup to her mouth, she took a long, reviving swallow.

'Hello, Jules.' She choked on her coffee, spraying the liquid all over the table, and suddenly a large hand was patting her on the back. 'I'm sorry if I startled you—that was not my intention.'

She could not believe her ears. Was she dreaming again? No...the deep voice stroking along her nerve endings and splintering them into a million shards of skin-tingling agitation was all too real—Rand Carducci.

Shoving back her chair, she leapt to her feet and spun around. 'You.' Open-mouthed, Jules stared incredulously at Rand; his hard, dark eyes were fixed on her with no apparent emotion at all. But suddenly she was aware that the hand patting her back had slipped around her waist and she was perilously close to his body. Involuntarily she raised a hand to his chest to ward him off. 'What are you doing here?' she demanded, shock holding her rigid.

'I am a guest of Peter Hatton. A dinner to confirm our business deal, done at my expense. I wanted to see you again. I arranged for your firm to do the catering,' Rand said in a clipped tone.

Not in her wildest, most erotic dreams of Rand had she imagined meeting him again like this...in a kitchen...hot and sweaty...and looking like something the cat had dragged in. It was only as the significance of his statement registered in her stunned mind that Jules noticed the immaculately tailored black dinner jacket, the red bow-tie and white silk shirt. And she wanted to scream and rage at him.

But she didn't. 'Bully for you,' she said mockingly, hanging onto her temper and her pride for grim death. All her earlier confidence that she was getting over Rand and the new hope for the business of a few hours ago demolished, in a few words by the man. Why had he gone to such lengths to see her? She didn't give a damn! It was enough to know he was still the same devious devil he had always been. 'Now get your hands off me, and get out of my kitchen.'

'Your kitchen?' One dark brow arched sardonically but at least his hand fell from her waist and he took a step back. 'I thought it was Hatton's.'

'You know what I mean,' Jules spat. 'You supercilious swine.' She made no attempt to hide her hostility, her eyes glittering with anger as she stared at him.

After what Pat had revealed to him Rand had felt terrible, and had walked into the kitchen prepared to apologise to Jules. But seeing her standing before him, her glorious red hair a tumbled mass around her shoulders, and with a damp tee shirt plastered to her magnificent, obviously braless breasts, and the contemptuous expression on her beautiful face, all his good intentions flew out of the window.

'Your opinion of me is the pits, so what the hell?' Rand swore thickly, and reached for her.

Caught off guard by the speed with which he moved, she raised her hands to push him away, but he jerked her against him so hard that her breath left her body, her hands trapped against his chest. She tried to twist away, but he held her against him, moulding her to his massive frame. Jules opened her mouth to protest, but his head swooped down and the fierce pressure of his mouth on hers cut the sound.

At the touch of his lips her pulse rate soared. She tried to resist, her hands flailed wildly at his chest, but she had ached for his touch for so long to her shame within seconds her hands stilled. She moaned deep in her throat, a hunger so intense it was torture raging through her, and her traitorous hands slid up over his shoulders, her fingers stroking feverishly through the silky black hair of his head. Instinctively she leaned into the hard heat of his body as the pressure went on and on, drowning in a huge wave of need that banished all thought of resistance from her mind.

Rand raised his head and looked down into her dazed green eyes, and, lifting a finger, he touched her bruised mouth. 'If I hurt you I am sorry.' And he did not just mean with the kiss, he meant for all that had gone on before. 'But, Jules, you and I need to talk.'

Shocked by her own response, Jules knew for the sake of her sanity all she needed was to get away and fast. 'No way,' she declared in a voice that shook, and with a mighty shove she broke free from his restraining arm and in a few speedy steps had put the width of the kitchen table between them.

'I have nothing to say to you.' Spying the invoice on the bench, she picked it up and flung it on the table. 'Except you owe me.' And she mentioned the sum of money. 'Everything is itemised, and I would prefer—' She was going to say cash, as she knew from bitter experience he had reneged on a cheque once before. But she never got the chance.

The kitchen door swung open. 'There you are, Rand. I thought you must have got lost.' Sir Peter Hatton walked into the kitchen. 'And you must be the chef.' He turned smiling grey eyes on Jules. 'My congratulations—you did a wonderful job, the meal was superb. And I would like to thank your lovely waitresses,' he ended with a smile.

'Thank you,' Jules responded with a shaky smile of her own for the tall white-haired gentleman. 'But they have already left.'

'Pity.' He chuckled. 'Come on, Rand, everyone else has gone and we don't want to delay the young lady's departure.' And with another smile for Jules he added, 'You must be tired.' Reaching for the bill, Peter Hatton picked it up, glanced at it and handed it to Rand. 'I trust you are going to add a hefty tip to that, Rand— you can afford it. Now how about a brandy in the study?'

Jules glanced at Rand, and his hard, intent stare played havoc with her nerves, the strength of purpose in those chilling depths sending a flicker of fear down her spine, but bravely she held his gaze.

'A gratuity for services rendered to a beautiful woman...' His dark eyes roamed over her in quite blatant male appreciation before he added, 'It goes without saying, and one who can cook so beautifully is a gem indeed.' Jules heard the pause and the mockery in his tone, and part of her was furious, while the other deplored her earlier helpless surrender to his kiss. 'And, yes, I will join you for a brandy, Peter.'

Thank God they were leaving… Jules suffered their goodnights and heaved a shaky sigh as the two men departed, her emotions in a state of flux, and the only thought in her head was to get away. She didn't give a damn if she never got paid; she wasn't stopping a second longer than the time it took her to clean up.

Coffee had been served in the large drawing room. And with feverish haste Jules dashed around collecting the final debris of the dinner party. Back in the kitchen she washed the last of the china and put it away; with a final glance around she gathered up her white jacket and stuffed it into the container along with the last few odds and ends, and shot out of the kitchen.

In record time she had deposited everything in the back of the car, and was behind the driving wheel. It was a bright moonlit night, but she was barely aware of her surroundings, her urge to flee paramount. Her hand shook uncontrollably as she pushed the key into the ignition, and turned on the engine…and in her haste she missed the gear and immediately stalled the car…

She didn't hear the passenger door open. 'Having trouble?' an all too familiar voice drawled mockingly. She turned her head and Rand was staring across at her.

'Only with you,' she yelled at him, so angry that she lurched across the seat to reach for the door-handle with every intention of slamming it in his face, but he caught her hand and slid into the passenger seat and she ended up sprawled half over him, her face in his lap.

Horribly conscious of the intimacy of her position, she placed her free hand on his thigh and struggled back into the driving seat, her face scarlet, and he caught hold of both her hands.

'Get out. Get out of my car,' she shrieked, and made a futile attempt to break free.

'Jules, *cara*, you didn't honestly think I was going to let you get away without our little talk, did you? And I have not paid you yet— not very businesslike,' he opined hardily.

'So send me a cheque, one with no strings attached this time,' she lashed back. For several seemingly endless seconds he stared at her, his dark eyes gleaming with an implacable intensity that sent a shudder down her spine, and suddenly she was afraid.

'I'll give you that crack, Jules, I deserved it,' he said quietly and pulled her hands closer. 'But we are still going to have a talk.'

With her hands imprisoned by his she was only inches from him. She felt his heat, the leashed strength of his powerful body, and every self-protective instinct she possessed warned her to beware. Rand was a formidable man determined to have his own way, whether she agreed or not, and experience had taught her he was at his most dangerous when he was being quiet and reasonable.

Clamping down on the anger bubbling inside her, Jules wondered what he could possibly want to talk to her about. And why now, two months since they had parted? She tried to free her hands again but his grip tightened, holding them pressed to her sides, his great body angled towards her.

'All right, talk,' she said curtly, bowing to the inevitable. She knew she was no match for his superior strength; far better to let him have his say, and get it over with.

'Not here—there is a lake not far from here I want you to see, so I will drive.' And in a flash he had bodily lifted her over into the passenger seat and was behind the wheel and by the time Jules managed to straighten up the car was moving down the drive.

She was so mad at his macho action, she grabbed his arm, and physically tried to pull his hand from the steering wheel. 'Stop the car, damn you!'

'Don't be an idiot,' Rand grated, and with impressive ease shook off her hand, one strong arm landing across her chest to restrain her. 'Remember Enrique—do you want to kill us both?'

His brutally blunt question, and the sudden awareness of what the friction of his arm was doing to her sensitive breasts, cooled her temper, but unfortunately not her body. Horrified by her own violent reaction, she sank back in her seat and pushed his arm away. 'No.'

In popular parlance Rand had all the attributes of 'a man to die for'. But although once she had harboured thoughts of loving him, she certainly wasn't dumb enough to die for him!

He slanted her a sardonic glance. 'Amazing—you do have some sense after all.'

# CHAPTER TEN

ARROGANT swine, Jules muttered under her breath, but sat in silence as he manoeuvred the car down the long drive and along a narrow road that meandered through a forest of trees.

'Have you ever been to a trout farm?' Rand asked as he drew the car to a halt.

'What?' The question was so unexpected, Jules' eyes flew wide and she looked around to see that the road had led to the edge of a large lake, the water shimmering silver in the moonlight. A small building of some kind stood on the shore, and part of the lake appeared to be sectioned off in big squares with either wood or metal, she wasn't sure. But she was sure the place was deserted, not a light or a human in sight, the only sound the occasional cry of some night animal.

Rand slid out of the car and walked around to open her door. 'Come on. As a chef it should interest you. You must have cooked dozens.'

'A trout farm.' She slid out of the car and looked up at him; he stood tall and vaguely forbidding silhouetted against the skyline. 'You want to talk about a trout farm?' Jules demanded, completely gobsmacked.

Rand looked down into her upturned face, and saw the incredulity in her brilliant eyes, and he had to smile. There was a faint breeze and it had swept a few long tendrils of hair across her beautiful face. 'No, Jules.' He lifted a finger and gently brushed the wayward hair back across her cheek and tucked it around her small ear, his heart thundering at the feel of her smooth skin against his fingertips. He wanted nothing more than to take her in his arms and kiss her senseless, but that was not why he had brought her here.

A shiver shook Jules' slender frame, but it had nothing to do with feeling cold, and more to do with the banked-down sensuality in his smile and the touch of his hand on her face. 'Then why?'

'Because Ester asked me to reiterate her invitation to you, and your mother if you like, to visit her in Italy,' he began cautiously.

Jules' green eyes widened to their fullest extent in amazement. Was he one stick short of a bundle or what? 'You didn't have to drag me out to a trout farm to tell me that. You could have told me in the kitchen. And as for visiting your stepmother, you must be joking—as the beneficiary of her brother's will she had to know you were selling the ranch, without the simple decency of telling me. My mother was right, we are better off having nothing to do with anyone connected to Carlos Diez. So you're wasting your time.'

Rand stiffened, his dark eyes narrowed angrily, not at all pleased at the slur on his stepmother, but then he realised with a wry grimace Jules was perfectly justified in thinking that way.

'There is more, and if you will hear me out you might change your mind. When we parted in Chile you were under the misapprehension I had sold the ranch to Señor Eiga behind your back, which was not the case at all.' Jules did not want to be reminded of Chile ever again but she did not have much option as Rand added, 'Walk with me and listen.'

He put his arm around her waist. She tried to shake it off, but he simply tightened his grip. 'The pebbles are difficult to walk on; stay calm and pay attention for once in your life. It is a long story and you should have been told at the time, but it was not my story to tell.'

Against her better judgment but intrigued by his words, Jules gave up the struggle and they strolled along the shoreline.

'You and Ester are not the only members of the Diez family left.' That didn't surprise Jules; a man like Carlos Diez had probably fathered children he didn't even know about. But what Rand said next captured her attention completely.

Sanchez was not just the manager of the ranch; he was the illegitimate half-brother to her late father. The information had been kept a secret between Carlos and Sanchez; not even Ester had known until after her brother's death.

In his position as executor, a week after the funeral Rand had been going through the family papers in the study at the hacienda and discovered a document proving Sanchez was the illegitimate son of the second Carlos Diez. He had asked Sanchez and he had admitted it was true. But he had also told Rand that, in a conversation he'd had with Carlos a month before he'd died, Carlos had told him quite bluntly he had thought of leaving a share of the ranch to him. But as Sanchez had been married to Donna for twenty years with no children, it was never going to happen now, so there was no point. Carlos was desperate for the Diez line to be continued not just for the present but also in the future, and as a last resort he had confided in Sanchez he'd even been considering it going through in his eyes the *lowly* female line...Jules. Which explained the codicil a few weeks later. It had been an attempt to ensure the continuation of Diez blood on the land he'd loved so much.

'That is incredible and so cruel to Sanchez!' Jules exclaimed, casting a shocked glance at Rand's hard-etched profile.

'Yes, but what was more incredible was the fact that within a month of the death of Carlos—Donna discovered she was pregnant.' Rand stopped and turned Jules to face him. 'Proof that miracles can happen,' he opined lightly. 'But even if she had not been I would have still done the same. I discussed the situation with Ester and, once she got over the shock she had a half-brother she had never met, she was in complete agreement that Sanchez should keep the ranch. After all, he has managed it for almost thirty years.'

'Poor Ester, she never had much luck with her family,' Jules murmured. 'But wait a minute—if that is the case, why did you not just tell me all this from the very beginning?'

'I wanted to, though to be blunt the way you ignored your father in his last weeks made me wonder if you would see the situation in the same generous way as Ester.'

'You mean you thought I was an uncaring daughter only out for what she could get.'

'Exactly,' Rand ruefully admitted. 'But that was not what stopped me. Contrary to what you implied earlier, Ester is a woman of the highest moral principles.' He cast her a wry glance. 'Stubbornness seems to be a family trait of the Diez gene pool. Because both Ester and Sanchez insisted I had to stick to your father's wish and give you the chance to fulfil the terms of the codicil if that was what you wanted. They flatly refused to let me tell you the truth until after the six months were up, in case it affected your decision in any way. Personally I thought they were being pig-headed.'

'You would—integrity does not strike me as one of your strong points,' Jules slotted in sarcastically.

Rand ignored her crack and continued. 'Think what you like. But they were adamant. I tried to tell them the codicil might not even stand up in court but they would have none of it.'

But Jules was barely listening to the detail as it slowly dawned on her. 'Sanchez is my uncle,' she said softly. 'I might have guessed—he was always so good to me, teaching me to ride, and trying to teach me Spanish.' She chuckled at the memory. 'He was the only man on the staff I really liked, and now I find out he is my uncle it is just incredible.' She turned shining eyes up to Rand. 'But marvellously incredible, and Donna is my aunt, and soon I will have a new cousin. I can hardly believe it,' she declared, a wide, beautiful smile illuminating her whole face.

'Believe it,' Rand said with a grin.

Suddenly she had an extended family, two people she was genuinely fond of, and the knowledge made her heart swell with joy. Then a sobering thought hit her. 'But if this is all true—' she frowned '—why on earth did you sell the ranch to Señor Eiga?'

'I didn't. A month after your father died, and after you had declared you wanted nothing to do with him or his estate, I approached Señor Eiga with a business proposition to buy his ranch. He agreed, with the stipulation he could live there for the rest of his life, not the other way around as you presumed.' Rand cast her a hard glance. 'Given his age and his only son dead, the arrangement suited him. But I could not legally complete the deal for six months because of the codicil. He and your father were right about one thing—it makes good business sense to amalgamate the two properties, and I am a businessman first and foremost. Sanchez will run the whole lot, and hopefully make an extremely healthy profit for all of us. I hope you agree.'

It was the exact opposite to what Jules had thought. Rand had bought Señor Eiga out, and she felt a complete fool; she had got the wrong end of the stick completely, and, mulling over what he had told her, she spoke without thinking. 'Now I see it all. I turned up and you did not trust me and were worried I would insist on marriage and then sell my share to someone else. Hence the sale option, so at worst the deal would be delayed a year, but would still go through,' Jules concluded, and met his compelling gaze with dignity.

'You did the right thing, Rand, I agree. It makes me very happy to think of Sanchez and Donna raising a family on the ranch; they belong there, and I never did. But I would like to know why you could not at least have told me I was wrong about the ranch at the airport when I was leaving,' she asked bluntly, 'instead of letting me think the worst.'

'Somehow I knew you would ask that and what can I say except I was angry?' Jules studied his dark features but was unable to read anything from his expression. 'I am not proud of how I behaved the week we were together, but I confess I never had any intention of complying with Carlos' request and marrying you. In fact I have no intention of ever marrying; I can't see the necessity.' He shrugged his broad shoulders eloquently as if to emphasise the point. 'But I was so furious that you never responded to any of my calls, I was sure you must be a heartless little gold-digger. Then when you arrived in Chile, so cool, so sophisticated and so uncaring of Carlos, and only after money, I was convinced.'

That he had actually thought her cool and sophisticated brought a glimmer of amusement to Jules' eyes—she had played her part better than she had thought—but her humour faded fast as he ploughed on.

'So I determined to string you along and get your acceptance for the sale without you knowing, while making sure you got as little money as possible, and for that I am truly sorry.' The corners of his mouth twisted wryly. 'Though the irony of you flatly refusing to marry me before I could say a word did not escape me.'

Jules searched his hard features, saw the conviction in his eyes and she knew he was telling the truth as he saw it.

She blinked slowly and her delight at knowing Sanchez was her uncle faded and a shiver shook her slender frame. She hugged her arms across her breasts in an attempt to stop trembling. She could understand his reasoning, but it was what he had *not* said that caused the pain in her heart: the realisation that he had made love to her countless times while disliking and distrusting her as a person.

However Rand tried to explain his actions, the truth was it could only have been that most base of emotions that had driven him to make love to her: sheer unadulterated lust...

Why was she surprised? she asked herself. She had always known if she was honest that as far as Rand was concerned finer feelings had never entered into the equation during their short-lived affair. Straightening her shoulders, she let her hands fall to her sides and walked back to the car.

Rand caught her arm. 'Jules, forgive me.'

She stopped. Rand asking forgiveness—that had to be one for the record books, she thought wryly. 'Sure,' she murmured and, lifting guarded green eyes to his, she saw the regret and something else she could not put a name to in his eyes. The silence between them stretched, fraught with a tension that was almost palpable, and then abruptly she looked away before his mesmerising gaze could seduce her all over again.

'Your explanation has been very enlightening, Rand, thank you. But it is all water under the bridge now, and I would like to get home. It has been a long, stressful day.' Congratulating herself on her cool, mature response, she suddenly sensed his inner rage as Rand murmured something viciously under his breath.

She took a quick step back, shocked by his fierce reaction. What had she said wrong now?

'Is that all you have to say? You have had a stressful day.' He raked a hand through his hair. 'How the hell do you think I feel?' He pinned her back against the car with his powerful body and cupped her head between his hands, holding her face up to his. 'Why didn't you tell me?' he demanded, staring down at her with glittering night-black eyes.

'I have no idea what you are talking about,' Jules snapped back, but inside she was quaking. She could sense the musky aroma of thoroughly aroused male and feel the powerful beat of his heart, and it took every ounce of will-power she possessed to withstand his blistering gaze.

'Try your mother, the lovely Liz who, according to Peter Hatton's cousin, Pat, had breast cancer the same as her. Liz who two months ago started a new expensive therapy only available at a private clinic at the same time as my dinner companion,' he said with biting sarcasm.

Jules' face paled, and she remembered her mother had mentioned Pat was at the dinner. 'So?' she said defiantly. 'My mother has nothing to do with you.'

'But she was the reason you wanted such a specific sum of money. My God, why didn't you tell me?' Rand asked, his features rigid with an emotion she could not quite discern. 'What had I ever done to you to make you believe you could not confide in me as your father's executor, the first time we met again in my office? We barely knew each other—I saw you a handful of times when you were a teenager, for heaven's sake! So where did you get the idea you could not trust me? Or did it please your masochistic little mind, after the way your father and Enrique had treated you, to think of me in the same unflattering light?'

'I did tell you my mother was ill,' Jules reminded him quietly. But deep down inside she knew there was some truth in his statement, and she felt slightly ashamed. Instead of playing the uncaring sophisticate she should have been more explicit at the time and trusted him with the real reason she'd wanted the money. It had been her own cowardice in facing up to the word *Cancer* that had stopped her, and her innate honesty forced her to admit her preconceived notion of the deviousness of men with any connection to her late father.

'Once. Just once you said your mother wasn't well, which implies a cold or the flu, and in your case I thought it was just an excuse. If I had known the real reason you could not respond to my calls to you…do you really think I would have been so…?'

'So what?' she asked tightly.

'So hard on you, Jules,' he conceded huskily, and she caught the deepening gleam in his dark eyes as his long body moved restlessly against hers making her achingly aware of just how hard he was.

'So callous as to seduce me, you mean,' she sneered, trying to shore up her weakening defences against the seductive pull of his all-powerful masculinity.

An expression of remorse crossed his hard face as a hand slipped down to her waist and drew her even closer.

'Do you have any idea how bad I felt tonight, when I realised what you had done, and why?' he confided bluntly. 'I was feeling stupid enough to start with, arranging the damn dinner when I should have had the guts to just call you, but after learning about your mother I felt about two inches tall.'

'A first for you, then.' Jules tried for humour, but he was not amused.

His eyes bored into her. 'It was for your mother's treatment, wasn't it?'

'Yes, but my mother knows nothing about it,' she hastened to explain. 'I didn't think she would accept money from my father, and she would be horrified if she knew I had asked for it.'

Rand's expression softened. 'She will never hear it from me, but take my advice and tell her. Your mother is also your business partner, and she is bound to wonder where the extra cash came from when she sees the year-end accounts. She will be hurt by your deceit, Jules, and you may well live to regret the omission. Take it from one who knows.'

Jules had been worrying about the same thing herself for the past few weeks, and was surprised by his perception. 'You're probably right.'

'Trust me on this, Jules, you are not a very good liar. If I had not been blinded by my own prejudices and sex—' a rueful smile curved his firm lips '—I would have seen through your pretence in Chile, and now I bitterly regret thinking even for a minute that you were only after money for yourself.'

Some of Jules' tension evaporated at Rand's quietly voiced admission and reassurance. She recognised it could not have been easy for a man with Rand's ego to admit he had made an error of judgment, and lifted her eyes to his, and for a long moment the only sound was the gentle lapping of water against the gravelled shore.

He stared at her with hypnotising intensity. Jules felt his great chest expand as he breathed deeply and the friction made her breasts swell in instant response, her nipples straining against the fabric of her tee shirt, the level of physical awareness vibrating between them making her tremble.

'But know this, Jules, I will never... ever...regret as long as I live making love to you,' he declared, his deep voice husky with emotion. 'It was only when you told me at the airport what you thought of me that I realised what I was losing, and I had to walk away because I also knew there was some truth in your words and felt ashamed. But if there is any chance we could renew our relationship...' And her stupid heart turned right over at the thought.

Jules saw his head move, and she knew what was going to happen. With a supreme effort of will she put up her hand to stop him. 'No, Rand.' For a heart-stopping second she saw the savage, primitive gleam in his eyes, she felt the tension in his body and as she watched he briefly closed his eyes, and, with a deep, harsh breath, he straightened up.

'I swore I would not do this,' he said harshly almost to himself, and stepped back, setting her free. 'Get in the car, and let's get out of here.' And in seconds he had bundled her into the vehicle and started the engine and was coolly asking her directions to the town.

'Wait a minute—this is my car. How will you get back to Hatton's?' Jules asked when she managed to get her brain in gear.

'I'll get a taxi,' he said without looking at her.

'There is no need for that. I'll drive and drop you off before I go home.'

'No, I insist on escorting you home.'

They were talking like two strangers, Jules thought sadly, but it was probably for the best. If the last hour had taught her anything it was that, much as she appreciated Rand telling her the truth about her father's estate, any further contact with him would be folly of the worst kind.

She closed her eyes for a moment, overcome by the intensity of her emotions; she had not got over Rand at all. From the moment he had kissed her in the kitchen and she had melted in his arms, as much a slave to his touch as she had been from their very first kiss, she had known... A few minutes ago it had taken every ounce of will-power she possessed to say no, and she knew it was his strength, his powerful control, and not hers, that had stopped him.

Finally she admitted what she had tried to deny from the first time they had made love together. She loved him and probably always would. But she was not a fool—he could not have made it plainer: he could switch his emotions on and off like a light socket, and he was not into commitment, that much was obvious. As for marriage, he had said earlier by the lake, 'I have no intention of ever marrying, I can't see the necessity.' Jules also realised she was the sort of woman who needed the whole nine yards.

'Jules. Which way now?'

She opened her eyes. Rand had stopped the car and was looking down at her a shade impatiently. She straightened up in the seat and, ignoring the pain in the region of her heart, she glanced out of the window and told him, 'Turn right here and it is the third house along.' It was only when he stopped the car outside the house that she realised she had another problem.

Jules slid out of the car and turned to find Rand was standing beside her, holding out her bunch of keys. 'Your keys, Jules, and if you don't mind could I use your telephone to call a taxi?'

She took the keyring from his outstretched hand and cast a panicked glance at the light beaming from the bay window of the living room. Her mother must still be up; no way did she want Rand to meet Liz. 'Surely you have a mobile?' she flung back, turning to look up at his unsmiling face.

'So gracious,' Rand said sardonically. 'But, no, I am afraid not, and, even if I did, do you seriously expect me to stand outside on the pavement—' he glanced at his wrist-watch, and then back at her worried face '—at eleven in the evening waiting heaven knows how long for a taxi?'

'But…I mean… Well…' Jules stammered to a halt. She saw the gleam of humour in his eyes, and felt like decking him. Instead, bowing to the inevitable, she took a deep steadying breath. 'No, of course not, but I think my mother is still up, and I don't want you upsetting her. So not one word about you, the money, or anything.'

'Don't be ridiculous, Jules.' He took her arm and urged her towards her own front door. 'You have to introduce me and, as you have probably mentioned the name of your father's executor, she will know who I am.'

Reaching the front step, Jules very reluctantly found the correct key and inserted it in the lock. 'Just watch what you say.' She slanted him a furious glance, and he met her anger with an expression of bland innocence on his attractive face that she didn't trust for a second. But she had no choice and, pushing open the door, she walked into the hall, a restraining hand on her arm, and Rand's head bent towards hers. 'Have no fear, Jules, I will be very diplomatic, and I promise I won't tell her we slept together.'

'You're late, darling,' her mother's voice rang out, and Jules walked into the living room, scarlet-faced, but before she could respond Rand swept past her and had done it for her.

'Blame me. Liz, isn't it?' He walked across to where her mother, wearing a pink dressing gown, was sitting on the sofa. 'We met earlier. But I did not realise who you were.' And he smiled down at her mother. 'You are as beautiful as Jules told me you were. Allow me to introduce myself.' And as Jules watched her mother rose from the armchair with a brilliant smile of feminine appreciation for the tall, dark, attractive man, and accepted the hand Rand offered. 'Rand Carducci—I'm sure Jules has told you about me.'

'Oh, yes,' Liz said, her smile fading to one of cool politeness at the mention of his name. 'Pleased to meet you, though you are not quite what I expected. Jules said you were middle-aged and going grey.'

'Really, Mother,' Jules protested weakly.

'Well, you did, darling.' And turning ice-green eyes on Rand, she added, 'Forgive my lapse in manners, but we don't usually have visitors so late. May I get you a drink?'

Jules knew her mother and she knew she was not pleased. 'It's okay, Mum, I bumped into Rand when I was clearing up. He had some news for me and insisted on driving home with me but refuses to let me drive him back to Hatton's so now he needs a taxi.'

'That does not surprise me. You look a very determined man, Mr Carducci. You were a friend of my late ex-husband, I believe.'

'I'll go and make that call,' Jules muttered and without looking at Rand she scuttled back into the hall and rang for a taxi. Three calls later she finally got a firm that could send a cab in ten minutes. Thank God, she thought as she put down the receiver, ten minutes wasn't too bad.

But slumped in the armchair two minutes later she began to feel it were a lifetime. Rand and her mother were sitting on the sofa about a foot apart and you could cut the atmosphere with a knife. Rand had already told Liz about Sanchez being Carlos' half-brother. Her mother had responded that she was not surprised, it was a trait of the Diez males to spread themselves around. But she did remember Sanchez and Donna as a pleasant couple.

Damned with faint praise sprang to mind...Jules thought, glancing at Liz, then Rand, then back again. Then Rand brought up the subject of visiting his stepmother, Ester, in Italy, at his expense of course.

'Thank you, that is very kind,' Liz said, 'but my health is not perfect yet and, to be honest, delighted as I am that Jules has other family besides me, I am not sure I want to get involved. My experience with her father rather put me off the Diez family.' Then turning her green eyes on Jules, she added, 'But Jules knows I am perfectly happy for her to keep in contact.'

Jules smiled rather weakly and was praying for the doorbell to ring.

'You do surprise me, Liz. After all, you are a Diez yourself; you have kept the Diez name,' Rand said smoothly.

'Only because Carlos would not give me a divorce unless I promised Jules kept his name, even if I married again. It was written into the proceedings. Though why he bothered when he virtually cut her out of his life, and his death it would seem, I will never know. Not that it bothers me; Jules and I have managed very well on our own, and I prefer it that way.'

'Mum.' Jules sat up straighter in the chair and looked at Rand. She saw the dark brows draw together and the tightening of his mouth, and she knew he was offended, and any second now he was going to tell her mother about the money he had given Jules. 'Mum, I think you—' And at that moment the doorbell rang.

'That must be the taxi. Get the door, Jules, darling,' Liz commanded.

Jules hesitated for a moment and then got to her feet. She wanted rid of Rand and she could talk to her mum later. 'Ready, Rand?' She glanced at him looking dark and broodingly attractive and she ached for him with a hunger she could barely control. She could not get him out fast enough.

'Yes.' He stood up. 'Goodnight, Liz, it has been interesting meeting you,' and followed Jules out of the room.

Jules had the front door open when Rand placed a hand on her shoulder. 'Walk with me to the taxi.'

She could feel the warmth of his body at her side, and the soft brush of his breath against her ear, and her stomach turned over. 'Yes, okay.' Anything to hasten his departure. She shot out of the house.

'I think I understand you a lot better now, Jules, after meeting your mother.' Rand stopped her headlong rush to where the taxi was parked at the roadside by grasping her shoulders and turning her around to face him. She tilted her head back, about to deny him, and her green eyes clashed with his and for some reason she could not tear her gaze away.

'Your mother is a very strong woman, and I believe she loved Carlos very much but she could never forgive him for betraying her, and she has nursed the bitter hurt for years. The really sad part is I believe Carlos loved her. Think about it—neither one of them ever married again. Perhaps now Carlos is dead Liz can start living again.'

'My mum loves life!' Jules exclaimed in astonishment. 'If she seemed a little cool, it is because it is late and she is tired, and she has been ill.'

'Maybe, but does she live it to the full?'

She opened her mouth to reply but nothing came out. Could Rand possibly be right?

'Don't let what happened between your parents colour your view on the rest of your family, Jules. Keep in touch with Sanchez and Donna; they would appreciate it. You have my number, give me a call when you can visit Ester in Italy and don't leave it too long.' And bending his dark head, he dropped a tender kiss on her softly parted lips, and was gone.

Back in the house Jules flopped down on the floor at her mother's feet. 'Some night, Mum, and some revelation; I have an uncle. How do you feel about that?'

'I love you, Jules, and I'm happy for you. But I got the distinct impression there was more going on between you and Rand Carducci than you told me.'

No way was she telling her mother about their affair, and, thinking quickly, Jules said, 'Well, I was not totally honest with you about my father's inheritance. It was not just a trophy but some money as well, and that is how we can afford your treatment.'

Her mother surprised her by responding with, 'Oh, that is marvellous. I was worried the cost might be a drain on the business.'

'You've changed your tune,' Jules said and then her mother's response surprised her.

'Why not? If the half-brother can inherit, then why shouldn't you have something?'

Over a cup of hot chocolate Jules brought up Rand's suggestion that they both visit Ester in Italy. 'What do you think, Mum?'

'My advice is the same as before: if you want to visit any member of the Diez family, feel free, the choice is yours, but be careful.'

Curling up in bed, Jules was relieved she had cleared the air with her mother, and she was quietly delighted that Sanchez was her uncle. But it was Rand who kept her from sleep. Much as she would like to meet Ester, she knew she would not. Because she dared not chance seeing Rand again. Having finally admitted to herself that she loved him, it ate at her heart that he could never be hers. He might enjoy sex with her if she let him, but as for exclusivity there was no chance, and, knowing herself, anything less would destroy her.

Saturday seemed interminable after making such an early start in the bakery and, serving in the shop, Jules longed for four o'clock to come so she could close up. She had let the rest of the staff leave at two-thirty, as she knew they only ever got a few late customers, especially when the weather was sunny like today. But now she was on her own it gave her time to think, and her thoughts were as usual of Rand. It had been five weeks since the last time she had seen him the night of the dinner party. She had written to Sanchez and Donna and had a lovely letter back. But she had not contacted Rand about visiting Ester because the thought of seeing him again, if only by accident, was too painful. But now she felt guilty.

She had arrived home yesterday afternoon and Jules' first shock had been when she'd walked in the house and seen her mum had had visitors. Her second shock had been when her mother had introduced them as Ester and Tony Carducci, and her third shock had been when she'd realised where her own auburn hair had come from. Ester at over sixty was going grey, but there was no mistaking the thick curling mass of auburn hair.

Rand's father was simply an older version of Rand in looks, but that was where the similarity ended. Tony Carducci was a doctor with a small thriving practice, and apparently that was how Ester had met him when she had gone to him for help when she'd first arrived in Italy after her terrible experience in a Chilean prison. He also seemed very quiet, or perhaps his English was not that good.

But over a very English afternoon tea Liz had prepared, Ester had been very voluble.

'Forgive me for turning up unannounced, Jules, but I could wait no longer. Your mother and I have already had a good talk and I fully understand her reluctance in the past to get involved with any member of Carlos' family, but happily we have sorted that out now.'

Then Ester went on to enthuse how marvellous it was about Sanchez, and Jules wholeheartedly agreed. She warmed to Ester as the older woman reminisced about her childhood days, and cleverly drew a mine of information from Jules about her own life, without her even noticing.

After tea Jules shared the sofa with Ester and just before they were going to leave Ester took Jules' hand in hers. 'Now tell me, child, what is the problem between you and my son? I may not be his natural mother, but I love him more than life and something is wrong.'

'Nothing to do with me, I am sure,' Jules said, embarrassed.

'Well, I am not so sure. I travelled here to see you but also because I am worried about Rand. I know Carlos and his codicil caused you a lot of trouble.' Jules shot a worried glance at her mother, hoping she could not hear. 'Don't worry, I have not mentioned it to Liz.' Ester squeezed Jules' hand sympathetically. 'But you cannot blame Rand for your father's deeds, and yet I have a feeling Rand thinks you do, and hence your reluctance to visit me.'

'I think you must be mistaken,' Jules said weakly.

'I don't think so, Jules, and I can't understand why you would have a problem now. I mean, in the end Rand sorted everything out to the benefit of us all. He sold that painting Carlos left him and with the cash from that and a lot of his own money he bought the neighbouring ranch and has set up what promises to be a very successful company. With Sanchez in charge it should make a handsome profit for all four of us, and Rand told me you were happy with the arrangement and agreed.'

'All four?' Jules queried faintly.

'Yes, Rand told you. Sanchez, Rand and you and I are all equal shareholders. I know I have only just met you, and from how Rand talks about you I don't believe for a moment you are greedy and want more.'

'No!' Jules exclaimed, horrified, as the import of Ester's words sank in. 'I was perfectly happy with you and, through you, Sanchez inheriting the lot. Your son never mentioned I was a shareholder or anything else. Quite frankly I don't care, and I would rather not talk about Rand.'

'Oh, my, the stupid man.' Ester sat back and nodded her head like a wise old owl, and then gave Jules a very peculiar smile. 'But no matter—you and Liz will still come and visit me in Italy.'

'I would love to,' Liz cut in. 'Unfortunately because of my treatment it would be difficult just now. But Jules could certainly visit.' And by the time the couple left Liz had fixed the date in two weeks' time. Jules, reeling from the shock of Ester's disclosure, hadn't the wit to object.

With an exasperated sigh Jules took off her apron; thinking about cancelling the trip to Italy was pointless as her mother was now determined Jules should go.

Jules took the money from the till, walked into the back room, and checked the last remaining bread and pastries were stacked at the back door, ready to be taken to the homeless hostel in the nearest city. She picked up her bag and dropped the takings inside. The bank and home, she thought, and headed back to the front shop. One last glance around, and she turned to leave but her way to the door was blocked.

She stared up at the man towering over her. Dressed casually in a sweater and jeans with a five o'clock shadow darkening his square jaw, he looked dishevelled and devastatingly attractive, and her heart turned over in her breast. 'Rand…I was just about to lock up,' she said nervously, colour rushing to her face.

'You should be locked up,' he snarled, his dark eyes blazing with fury figuratively shrivelling her to a crisp. 'Because of you Ester persuaded my father to fly her halfway across Europe and back. I only found out about it this morning and when I tackled her *she* was furious with *me*. Where the hell do you get off calling me a liar to my own mother?'

Jules took a step back and came up hard against the counter. 'I never,' she murmured.

'Liar.' He grabbed her by the arm and pulled her behind him into the back shop. 'I have been far too careful with you.' Spinning her around, he hauled her into his arms and kissed her with a savage hunger, more punishment than passion, but even so in seconds Jules was weak at the knees with her pulse racing like a high-speed train.

Rand lifted his head and drew in a deep, rasping breath. 'Why did you do it, Jules? Why deny knowing you were a shareholder in the company, pretend I had cut you out of the estate—what possible reason could you have? Or was it just your pathological dislike of any man who knew your father?' he demanded.

'But you never told me,' she said. 'Or if you did I never heard you.' She read anger in his eyes and a hardness that shook her, and then he grasped her chin and tilted her face up to his, looking long and deep into her dazed green eyes.

Harshly he said, 'I told you at the lake. I had amalgamated the two ranches, and Sanchez would run the lot, and hopefully make an extremely healthy profit for *all* of us. I asked you if you agreed and you said yes. What part of that did you not understand?' he asked.

'Oh, I remember you saying that.' She saw rage about to leap in his eyes and rushed on. 'But it never entered my head you meant me. I thought by us you were referring to Sanchez, Ester and yourself. After all, in Chile when you gave me the money you said it was a final payment.'

Rand turned pale beneath his tan and stared at her for several long seconds before he said, 'I can see now how you might think that way. I had certainly given you enough reason to think that badly of me. What can I say?' He spread his hands wide and took a step back. 'I'm sorry, Jules.' His hands fell to his sides. 'Apologising to you is fast becoming a habit with me.'

'I don't mind. I think I could get to like it,' she said with a smile of relief that he had got over his anger.

Rand moved closer and studied her delicate features, his eyes hooded. 'Could you get to like me, Jules?' he asked quietly. 'Could we

possibly start again? Would you at least try?'
he ended, his deep voice husky with emotion.

Jules' mouth went dry and she could hear
her heart beating wildly as she wondered if she
dared take a chance. After three months without him, she didn't really have a choice. 'I
think I could be persuaded,' she said softly.

'Ah, Jules.' Rand reached for her and
tugged her gently against his hard body, and
this time as his mouth covered hers she welcomed him.

Jules sat in the passenger seat of the red sports
car as Rand manoeuvred it through the
Saturday afternoon traffic that clogged the
streets of Rome and thought of how two short
weeks ago she had been stuck in the shop wondering how she could get out of visiting Rome,
then Rand had appeared. She had ended up
going out to dinner with him and back to his
hotel. Thinking about it now brought a smile
to her face, and idly she stroked his hard, masculine thigh, a long, contented sigh escaping
her.

'A penny for them?' Rand asked, hearing
her sigh.

'I was just wondering what I am going to say to your mum at dinner tonight when they ask me which ancient wonders of Rome I have seen today.' She turned her head slightly and studied Rand's striking profile. 'Somehow I don't think a glimpse of the Coliseum from the inside of a hotel bedroom will go down too well,' she teased.

'I didn't hear you complaining at the time.' He slanted her a wicked grin, and laughed out loud at the blush that suffused her face.

'You're shameless,' Jules gasped.

'And you love it,' Rand declared with outrageous masculine conceit. They had spent the past five hours making incredible love, Jules was the most wildly responsive woman he had ever known and yet she still blushed, she fascinated him, and he had never felt better in his life, but he could not resist teasing her.

He was right, Jules conceded, but she was not about to tell him that. Since their last meeting in England, Rand had called her every day, and Jules had been counting the hours until her departure for Ester's home in Rome, and meeting him again.

She had arrived last night, and Rand had met her at the airport and driven her to his parents' home. The Carducci house was a lovely old villa on the outskirts of Rome. Inside it was warm and welcoming and perfectly preserved with a generous garden and terrace.

Last night over a meal served outside on the terrace the conversation and the wine had flowed freely, and when Ester had suggested a sightseeing trip to the centre of Rome the next day Rand had intervened.

'Given, Mamma, you are not a hundred per cent fit, and I have the weekend free, how about I act as Jules' guide for the day? And I will bring her back early for dinner...'

His father supported the idea, as did Ester. But even more amazingly, when Rand then suggested he could free up a few days next week and take Jules on a driving tour to show her more of the Italian countryside, his parents agreed again.

# CHAPTER ELEVEN

'SLEEPING beauty, wake up, or you're going to burn.'

Jules' long lashes fluttered against her cheek, her eyes opened and slowly focused on the tall, bronzed body of Rand, wearing a pair of brief black swimming trunks, and nothing else. 'Adonis personified,' she murmured, her soft green gaze lifting to his ruggedly attractive face, a sultry smile curving her lips.

'Thank you, *cara mia*, and now *I* am burning.' Rand's eyes darkened as they trawled over every luscious inch of her incredible body displayed to perfection in a tiny white bikini. 'That bikini should be X-rated.'

Jules stretched languorously, her green eyes connecting with his. 'You bought it for me,' she reminded him.

'I must have been mad.' He reached a hand out to her. 'I'd kill any other man who looked at you wearing that.'

She placed her hand in his. 'For your eyes only, hmm?' she prompted as he pulled her to her feet. Secretly adding his possessive comment to her growing 'hope for love' list.

'You better believe it, Jules.' He lifted her hand to his mouth and kissed the centre of her palm, and her heart soared.

She wanted to pinch herself, to make sure this was real, her gaze winging around the magnificent setting. Their driving tour had been a direct route to Rand's own house and it was magnificent. The deep blue of the oval-shaped swimming pool set in a mosaic-tiled surround was designed to look like a gigantic eye. She had laughed when she had first seen it two days ago when they had arrived, and she had been smiling ever since.

She looked back up into Rand's striking face. 'I'm flattered.' She rested her hands on the slope of his hips. 'But what are you doing out here? I thought you said you had some work to catch up on.'

'I changed my mind.' His fingers twisted in the tiny bow between her breasts, her top parted and he flicked the straps off her shoulders so she was standing before him, her high, firm breasts revealed to his glittering gaze. 'I saw you from the study window.' His hands cupped the creamy mounds, and Jules dragged in an unsteady breath. 'And I told myself I would join you for a swim, and make sure you did not burn.' His thumbs grazed her burgeoning nipples. 'But in reality all I can think of is this.' And his head dipped down.

Jules swayed back, her fingers digging into his waist and she groaned her pleasure as with tongue and teeth he teased her taut nipples.

'You like that,' Rand murmured against her skin, trailing tiny kisses up to her throat and finally to her lips. 'My sweet, sexy Jules.' His hand slipped down to cup her bottom and pull her into the hard heat of his aroused body. 'And so do I.' His black eyes, gleaming with sensual amusement, burned into hers, and she deliberately let her hand dip to his trunks and stroke him free. She felt his body jerk and she smiled back.

'So it would seem,' she teased. 'You are a very decadent man, Rand Carducci.' And she stroked him some more. 'Stripping me half naked in broad daylight.' She watched as his skin tautened across his high cheekbones, saw his heavy-lidded eyes almost close, and she heard him moan and gloried in the sound. 'It is only fair I should do the same,' she murmured, and her tongue darted out to lick the strong column of his throat, and lower to his chest...

'No.' Rand suddenly grasped her by the upper arms and lifted her away from him, his great chest heaving. 'You have been out long enough, you are too fair for sex in the sun.' Swinging her up in his arms, he carried her into the villa and straight to the bedroom.

'Rand, don't,' she shrieked as he playfully swung her shoulder-high and dropped her from a great height onto the bed, and she was still bouncing on the mattress when he leapt on top of her.

'Rand...' she gasped again as he pinned her beneath him, and kissed her breathless, his mouth hard, hot and hungry and driving her wild with wanting, while his hands deftly removed their last scraps of clothing.

He lifted up on one arm, his smouldering dark eyes dancing with wicked humour. 'So you don't want to play, my lovely.' He rubbed a finger and thumb together, twisting an imaginary moustache like a villain from an old silent movie. 'Then I must persuade you,' he growled.

Jules burst out laughing, and in that moment she knew she would never love another man in her life the way she loved Rand. The sombre-suited man, the playful, passionate lover, he was everything to her, and she felt her heart swell with such emotion she had to close her eyes to hide the tears that threatened.

'Do you wish to play dumb, fair maiden?'

Her eyes flew open as his mouth closed over the hard peak of one swelling breast, and ripples of sensation shot down to the apex of her thighs. With hands and lips he travelled a tormenting path from her breasts to her belly and lower.

She clutched wildly at his broad shoulders, and his head lifted towards her, his incredibly molten black eyes flicked to hers, demanding and promising, and then she was engulfed in a fireball of sensation as he found the pulsating centre of her sexuality. She was conscious of nothing but the incredible mindless excitement as he sent her swirling hotter and higher until she was almost at screaming-point.

He moved up and over her in one fluid movement and thrust into her and she cried his name, her body clenching on a possession so hard and deep that she came in an instant tumultuous release, fingers digging into his flesh, and then slowly relaxing.

But Rand did not stop. His hand slipped up her spine and lifted, his dark head bent to her breast and his mouth suckled the still proud peak to the rhythm of the thrusting drive of his magnificent body and in seconds Jules was spiralling up out of control again. She felt his every muscle clenching taut and then the second climax hit her as Rand's great body shuddered violently in a paroxysm of release.

'I'm too heavy for you,' Rand husked and withdrew when the lingering aftermath of sensation finally subsided, and pushed up.

'Hot and heavy,' she gasped and stretched up and linked her hands around his neck, her lustrous green eyes smiling into his. 'It just gets better and better,' Jules murmured breathlessly.

'It could be better still,' Rand said softly, and, resting on his forearms either side of her body, he added, 'You could move in with me.'

'Here, you mean?' Jules was stunned and her hands fell from his neck and she stared up at him, hope blossoming in her heart. He was offering her the commitment she longed for, or was he…?

'Where else? It is my home,' he opined lightly. 'And you do like the house, you have told me so over and over again.'

'Well, yes.' Jules felt as though she were feeling her way through a minefield. She could not bear the thought of losing Rand, but was this a roundabout way of proposing, or was he offering a temporary arrangement?

'Great.' And then he buried his hands in her hair and kissed her, and in moments she was dizzy and disorientated all over again.

Rand was all macho determination when he rolled off her and sat up, pulling her up into his arms. 'I will go back to England when you leave in three days' time and collect your things. It shouldn't take more than a day.'

'Wait a minute.' Jules pushed out of his arms, and, pulling the edge of the sheet over her naked breasts, she turned to look at him. 'I didn't mean yes I would move in with you, Rand, I meant, yes I love your house.' She glanced around the huge elegant bedroom. 'Who wouldn't?' She looked back at him. 'But that is not the point. I can't just up sticks and move to Italy at the drop of a hat. I have a business to run.'

'I can easily take care of that,' Rand said dismissively.

'How, exactly?' Jules asked slowly.

'I'll get my personnel department to look for a replacement chef for you, and my people will keep a check on the business side of things, hire someone else so your mother does not have to work at all unless she wants to. Your business will be fine, and waiting for you if you want to resume work at some future date.'

She listened with mounting dismay as he spelt out his brilliant plan, and by the time he had finished she had slipped off the bed and was standing looking down at his smiling, arrogant face with anger in her heart. She felt like hitting him, but instead she said, 'And what exactly would I be doing, when your hired hands have taken over my work commitments, Rand?'

Rand flung his long legs over the bed and stood up. 'You will be with me, of course.

When I have to travel on business you will come with me; it will be perfect.' He reached for her, but Jules took a step back.

'What's the matter with you, Jules? I thought you would be pleased.' A frown of raw impatience twisted his rugged features. 'You can't possibly live with your mother all your life; you have to spread your wings some time and leave home. Just think about it—we could be together every night. My proposition makes sense and you know it.'

Proposition, not proposal... He had even offered to keep her business running so when he'd had enough of her she would have something to go back to. How generous, she thought scathingly, lowering her thick lashes to veil her expressive eyes so he would not see the anger and bitter disappointment she felt.

'Be sensible, Jules, you know you want to.' He reached for her and pulled her to him, his hand splaying across the base of her spine, and his other tipping up her chin. 'So what do you say? Will you be my live-in lover...lover?' His dark eyes gleamed with amusement and something more, and suddenly Jules was very aware of their naked state, and she was tempted...oh, so tempted…much against her better judgment.

A host of different questions flooded through her mind, the most important—could she bear to lose him? She loved him with all her heart, and held close in his embrace she queried if what Rand was offering was all that bad in this day and age. In time he might come to love her; should she take the chance?

She studied his hard, attractive face, and felt herself weakening, but this decision was too important for her to be diverted by sex. 'Have you lived with many women?' She needed to know if she was to be just one in a long line.

'None at all,' he confessed. 'I never felt the need.' His lips twisted in a wry smile. 'The women I knew before you tended to track me down.'

'Your arrogance is showing again.' Jules chuckled, feeling a vast sense of relief; if she was the first then there was hope she might, with luck and love, be the last. 'But what about Maria—you were engaged to her.'

She felt his great body tense, his hands falling abruptly from her body, and he turned away. Dropped like a hot potato sprang to mind... Surprised her innocuous question could cause such a reaction, she watched him pick up his robe from the bed and pull it on, then slowly he turned back to face her, his dark gaze chillingly cold. In the space of a few minutes he had switched from eager lover to ice man.

'Don't ever mention Maria's name in my presence again,' he said curtly.

His command split her heart like a rapier, destroying all hope as the realisation hit her. Rand loved Maria, always had and always would.

She brushed past him and picked up her robe and slipped it on, her mind spinning in ever-widening circles of despair. How had she been so dumb to think he might care for her? He wanted her for sex, nothing else. The truth was she would be no more than a mistress to be paid off when he tired of her, and the realisation made her sick to her stomach.

She had almost convinced herself to move in with him, and hope love would grow. But there was no hope when he loved another woman and had done for years. She turned back to see him striding towards the door, and suddenly the hurt, the injustice of it welled up inside her. The only two men she had thought she loved had both loved the same woman, and it was not, nor ever had been, Jules, and that was when she lost it…

'Have no fear, Rand,' she flung at his departing back, tightening the belt of her robe, her body shaking in reaction. 'You will never hear me mention your precious Maria again. Because you will never see me again.'

Rand spun around on his heel, bristling with anger, and she watched him stride towards her, but she didn't care. 'Turned you down in the end, did she? Well, I'm not surprised, she never gave a hoot for you anyway.'

Rand's hand rose and she thought he was going to strike her, his eyes leaping with rage. But with supreme control his hand stopped mid-air and he raked his fingers through his hair instead. 'No. I have never hit a woman and I am not going to start with you. But Señor Eiga was right about you; you really are a hard-hearted bitch.'

Jules paled at his brutal opinion of her, but as he continued her fury grew. 'Enrique might have made one mistake, poor sod. But he loved and revered you and he was devastated when you ran out on him and his depression cost him his life in the end and—'

Her magnificent green eyes flashed as her temper finally exploded and she cut him off with, 'Why, you stupid, sanctimonious pig. Your friend Señor Eiga tell you that, did he?' She heard his hissed intake of breath; he had not expected her to retaliate. 'Well, let me tell you, if Enrique was depressed over anyone, it wasn't me. Ask your precious Maria. Who did you think I found him rolling around with stark naked? They had been lovers from the age of fourteen. If anyone is a poor sod it is you for still loving the woman. The only thing that surprises me is that you did not marry her years ago, because, according to your sainted fiancée, Maria, Enrique loved her and wanted to marry her, but she thought you were a better bet. She did not want to be stuck on a ranch when she could travel the world with a wealthy man.'

His face was like carved stone, his eyes black and bitter as he watched her spilling out the angry words and continued to stare at her as though he had never seen her before, the tension mounting in the lengthening silence.

'Nothing to say, Rand? The truth hurt?' Jules mocked.

His dark eyes curiously blank, he stared down at her. 'How dare you speak ill, lie about the dead?'

'Oh, don't give me that holier-than-thou routine. Enrique is long gone.' She thought bitterly of the other woman. It was not her Rand wanted, he was merely using her and that hurt. Tortured by jealousy, she added, 'If you don't believe me, then go and ask Maria. Though I gather she must have dumped you anyway, and I can't say I blame her.'

He gave her one look, his face wearing a hard remoteness that was somehow frightening in itself. 'You bitch,' he said between clenched teeth. 'Maria is dead, as you well know.'

All her anger and jealousy whooshed out of her like a spent balloon. 'Oh, no—when? How?' she murmured, her eyes widening in shocked horror on his.

'*Dio*, you are some actress.' Rand shook his head in disgust. 'Don't pretend you don't know. You told me yourself Señor Eiga wrote to you about the accident, and Maria was in the car with Enrique.'

'He never mentioned it,' Jules murmured to herself. 'It was one line, ''Enrique crashed his car and died because of you, I hope you rot in hell.'''

She looked up at Rand. He stood towering over her, his face grey beneath his tan, and she saw him flinch as though she had struck him. But she did not care any more; all her hopes and dreams of love were shattered once and for all.

'Obviously renewing our affair was a monumental mistake.' And she had made it, Jules knew with sickening certainty, and stood up.

It had been bad enough when he'd thought she was only after money. She glanced back at the rumpled sheets and wanted to weep. Every time they had made love, he had been harbouring the thought that she was indirectly responsible for the death of the woman he had loved—it was unthinkable! She felt his hand settle on her arm and she shrugged it off without looking at him. 'I need a shower.'

There was a silence in which she walked across to the bathroom, and closed and locked the door behind her. She shrugged off her robe, and stepped into the shower cubicle, turned on the tap, and only then did she give way to her tears.

Rand gunned the motor of the sports car and took the twists and turns of the coastal road at breakneck speed. It was only when he narrowly missed an oncoming fruit lorry that he came to his senses and slowed down, and finally he turned and drove back towards his house. He had bought a smallholding of some twenty acres and had the house built specifically to his requirements with a magnificent view over the sea, but he drove past the entrance to his drive and on to where the old farm buildings stood. He parked the car and roamed restlessly around. He was having them renovated and they were just about finished. As was his relationship with Jules, and the bitter irony of the thought made him groan.

Deep down he had known as soon as she'd told him about Maria and Enrique that she'd been telling the truth, but he'd been so enraged at the thought of being cuckolded by the pair of them he had vented his fury on Jules, yet if anyone was the innocent party in the whole affair it was her.

It all made sense. He had been engaged to Maria for almost five years, and, though the sex between them had been good, it had not been very often, happening only during the three or four weeks of the year when he'd visited Chile.

He had loved her in a way, but, being brutally honest, he had been much more interested in expanding his business interests than he had been in getting married. Half of the attraction had been the fact Maria had been trying to build a music career and as long as he'd helped out with cash she hadn't hassled him. It had been convenient for both of them at the time.

But with hindsight he realised Maria had been in no great hurry to marry him either. Tellingly he realised Maria had only started pressing for a date for the wedding after Jules had left Enrique. Probably because once Jules had gone and his father's plans for the ranch had been shot Enrique had been pressuring Maria to marry him instead.

It put a whole new complexion on the car crash; two lovers quarrelling while driving at speed was a much more likely scenario. Hadn't he and Jules done much the same thing after Hatton's dinner? But at least he had been driving slowly at the time.

No wonder Jules had wanted nothing to do with the Diez ranch. The place and the people had caused her nothing but heartache and she had been little more than a child at the time.

He sank down on the ground and rested his back against a gnarled old olive tree. His own behaviour since he'd met Jules again a few months ago had been diabolical when he thought about it now, and after this afternoon's argument she was never going to speak to him again.

He rested his head back against the tree, and wondered, without conceit, how a brilliant, intelligent, articulate man such as himself could behave as a boorish, thick-headed dolt with the one woman in the world he cared about—Jules.

Because she was the one woman in the world he cared about… He had his answer and, leaping to his feet, a look of grim determination on his face, he climbed back into the car and drove off.

\*     \*     \*

Jules quoted her credit card number over the phone and replaced the receiver, muttering 'Patronising twit.' Of course she knew it was the holiday season, but she was not happy; the earliest flight she could get back to England was tomorrow evening at ten.

'You stay in for dinner?' Rand's manservant, Tomas, who had been out for the day, suddenly appeared from the back of the house.

'Yes,' Jules said with a grim smile. She knew it would be nearly impossible to find a hotel room in Rome this late in the day. And she was not prepared to spend the next thirty hours hanging around an airport. Rand had caused her enough pain and discomfort already in her life, but not any more. 'About eight would be fine, Tomas,' she said firmly and he nodded his head in acceptance and disappeared back into the kitchen.

Jules felt like disappearing, but her pride would not let her run away. She wouldn't give Rand the satisfaction, and slowly she walked back upstairs. She had already packed all of her things and moved them into one of the spare bedrooms. She was back in control of her life; no more bending like a willow in the wind to Rand's every whim.

Entering the bedroom she had commandeered as her own, Jules kicked off her sandals and flopped down on the bed. She wasn't budging until dinnertime; she had no desire to see Rand before she had to. Walking down the staircase at a minute to eight, casually dressed in white hipster trousers and a mint-green cotton top that left her midriff bare, Jules wondered if Rand would even appear. She had heard him roar off in his car hours ago, and frankly she didn't care if he crashed the red monster.

Tomas told her they were dining outside and she stepped out through the huge plate-glass doors and drew in a deep breath of the warm scented night air.

He was waiting for her on the patio where a table was set for dinner. Casually dressed in cream chinos and a short-sleeved shirt open at the neck with a button-down collar, tall and dark and incredibly attractive, he watched her approach. Her traitorous heart skipped a beat and she swiftly diverted her attention to the table.

'I wasn't sure you would still be here,' Rand said softly.

She contrived a casual shrug. 'I have no desire to go back to your parents' home, and the first flight I could get is for ten tomorrow evening.' She glanced back at the elegant sprawling white house. 'But I see no reason to spend over a day hanging around an airport when this place is big enough to accommodate both of us without our ever meeting. After all, we are both mature adults; the end of a brief affair is no big deal.'

'Very sensible, Jules, sit down and allow me to pour you a drink. This is a rather good Barolo,' Rand said. 'And I know you like red wine.'

She sat down and accepted the glass of wine he handed her, thinking, keep calm, keep focused and she would be out of here tomorrow at least with pride intact.

Tomas appeared with the food and she heaved a silent sigh of relief and to her surprise she discovered she was really hungry. But then she had missed lunch, and the reason why brought a pink tinge to her cheeks.

She finished off the first course of grilled langoustine and glanced across the table at Rand. He was unusually quiet, but then why not? At the end of an affair there was not much to say, and she started on the second course of veal marsala with less enthusiasm, the steadily thickening tension in the atmosphere between them killing her appetite.

'More wine?' He sent her a brief smile.

'Yes, thank you.' She watched him fill her glass and then fill his own and, lifting it to his lips, drain the contents and set it down on the table.

For some reason Jules realised it was Rand who was the more uncomfortable of the two of them. She glanced at the wine bottle—it was empty—and then across the table at Rand. 'You must really like this wine; you've drunk almost the whole bottle,' she said tightly.

He tautened perceptibly, his narrowed dark eyes resting on her with grim intensity. 'And do you blame me after your revelation this afternoon?'

'I told you the truth.' She placed her cutlery back on the table; she had had enough to eat and enough of this farce of a meal.

'I know. Once I got over the shock it all made perfect sense.'

Jules gave him a puzzled look, disconcerted by his response.

'You were right, Maria was never eager to marry me,' he said quietly. 'As for her and Enrique, it was so obvious when I cast my mind back. They were great friends when I first met her; I even asked Enrique to look after her when I was away.' Rand gave a hard laugh and pushed his plate away. 'What a joke.'

Jules could sense his anger and his pain and almost felt sorry for him.

'They didn't deserve to die, but I can't pretend I am sorry they are gone.' There was something so cold and cynical about Rand's attitude, Jules' pity vanished. 'My only regret is you at such a young age had to be dragged into such a sorry saga.'

'Yes, well, it is all over now,' Jules said flatly. She should have felt triumphant Rand believed her, but she didn't. Because it did not alter the fact he had loved Maria and he didn't love Jules. She was wasting her time living in hope. She knew she wasn't cut out to play the sophisticate mistress, or lover. It wasn't worth the pain, the betrayal of her own ideals and morals, and eventually it would destroy her. 'And now, if you will excuse me,' she said, coolly polite, and rose to her feet.

'No.' Rand leapt to his feet and sent the table crashing to the ground, crockery and cutlery flying everywhere. Then his sensual mouth tightened in a grim, bloodless line, his piercing black eyes capturing and holding her shocked gaze. 'Jules, to employ your own words, will you excuse me?' And, stepping over the debris on the ground, he grasped her slender shoulders. 'And will you marry me?'

If Rand had not been holding her she would have collapsed at his feet in shock. Wide-eyed, she stared at him, unable to believe what he had said.

Tomas appeared, probably having heard the table crash, but Rand said something in quick-fire Italian and he left, but without Rand ever taking his eyes off Jules. 'Will you marry me, Jules?' he repeated with steely determination. 'Forget about what I said this afternoon; forget about everything but you and I.'

It was her dream come true, but too late, Jules realised sadly. If she ever married she wanted a husband who loved her and only her; she was not prepared to come second best, not even for Rand. 'No. Sorry.'

'Why not?' Rand demanded with savage ferocity, his glittering black eyes blazing into hers. 'You know we are good together.'

'I know, but I also know you love Maria, always have and always will,' Jules said softly, 'and I can't compete with a ghost.'

'A ghost...Maria?' Rand echoed incredulously. 'I never loved Maria. I have made love to you more in the couple of weeks we have actually spent together than I ever did with Maria in as many years.'

'Sex,' Jules snapped. It was so typical of Rand.

'No, yes,' Rand thundered, '*Dio!* I am making a mess of this.' One hand dropped from her shoulders to loop around her waist. 'I didn't mean sex. I meant love. I love you, Jules.'

Held close against his magnificent body and with his eyes burning into hers with an intensity of feeling he made no attempt to hide, Jules felt hope unfurling inside her. He had said the words 'I love you', the words she had longed to hear, but she was still afraid to trust him. 'But you were engaged to be married,' she could not help murmuring.

'I know, and though it shames me to say it I never loved Maria—not the way a man should love the woman he wants for a wife. Not the way I love you. You know me, Jules, I can't keep my hands off you.' And to illustrate his point the hand on her shoulder moved to trace the soft swell of her breasts revealed by her low-cut top.

With her nipples hardening in clear relief against the soft cotton, and heat curling her stomach, Jules said breathlessly, 'That proves nothing.'

'It proves I want you quite madly. Do you honestly think I would put up with a long-distance relationship like the one I had with Maria if I had really loved her? I was young and attracted by a pretty face in a nightclub, bedded her, and got engaged on an impulse. It only lasted as long as it did because it suited Maria while she pursued her singing career and it suited me probably because she was so undemanding. When it did cross my mind that the relationship wasn't going anywhere, I did not want to hurt Maria by breaking it off. I was probably too young and too much of a gentleman.'

She didn't know what to believe. 'You may be a gentleman—' she resorted to mockery '—but you never have any trouble telling me exactly what you think.'

Rand winced as her jibe hit home. 'You're right but, to be brutally honest, I was working flat out to set up my business, and I thought Maria would make as good a wife as any eventually.' Rand tightened his fingers splaying across her bare midriff. 'Surely that tells you something, Jules. I never believed in love until I met you.'

Jules looked up at him unable to speak, unable to feel anything but a wild, familiar happiness building up inside her.

'Jules, come into the house,' he said tautly, and she allowed him to lead her into the elegant salon and seat her on the sofa. She watched as he crossed the room and poured himself a large brandy and downed it in one go, her own emotions in such a state of chaos she couldn't think straight.

'I am not doing this well at all.' Rand raked a hand through his hair, sending it all over his brow. 'But you have got to believe me, Jules.' He crossed and sat down beside her and, taking one of her hands in his, 'I love you and I want to marry you.' And to her utter and complete astonishment he withdrew a small box from his trouser pocket and opened it. Her eyes were fixated on the brilliant emerald and diamond ring in the bed of velvet, her heartbeat accelerating. He really did want to marry her, and tears stung her eyes. She looked up into his dark face, saw the sincerity and love and, surprisingly for Rand, a glimmer of uncertainty.

'You bought the ring for me?' she queried in a voice that shook with emotion. 'But this afternoon...'

'This afternoon I was an idiot,' Rand said tautly. 'I was under a lot of strain, I was determined to ask you to move in with me but I was scared that you would refuse, and then I was scared if you did you might leave me a few months later.' Rand afraid was a whole new concept for Jules and she watched him with shining eyes as he continued. 'After all, both you and your mother ran away from men you had made a commitment to, so I wasn't exactly confident.'

'You not confident?' Jules smiled at the absurdity but she saw the flash of vulnerability in his eyes, and her heart turned over with love. He really had been afraid, and she realised he was just as prone to emotional uncertainty as she was herself.

'I got over it quickly after making a complete ass of myself when you told me about Enrique and Maria. I drove off in a rage and then I stopped and thought for a while down by the old farm buildings. Then drove off again to the nearest jeweller's.' He took the ring out of the box, and, looking deep into her brilliant green eyes, he slipped the ring on the third finger of her hand. 'You will marry me, Jules, because I won't take no for an answer, and I will make you love me if it takes the rest of my life.' The old arrogant Rand was back with a vengeance.

'Yes and I already do,' Jules said disjointedly, dizzy with happiness.

Rand groaned something in Italian, and lifted her hand to his mouth and kissed the ring like a benediction. 'I never believed I could love anyone the way I love you.'

Jules curved her hand around his jaw line, her brilliant eyes gazing into the smouldering, possessive black of his. 'You excite me, infuriate me and madden me, but I fell in love with you the first time you kissed me.'

'Now she tells me,' Rand growled and swung her up in his arms and kissed her passionately as he carried her upstairs. 'I feel as though I have waited all my life just to love you.' And he kissed her again and lowered her gently down on the bed.

She reached up to him, and pulled him down beside her. 'And when did you realise you loved me?' she asked him between kisses.

'I should say this afternoon at the farmhouse, but that is not strictly true,' he admitted ruefully. 'I think I have known for months but did not want to admit it. Probably from the moment I set eyes on you again. I remembered you from the past as a pale-skinned slender kid with huge green eyes who looked far too young to be thinking of marriage and I felt rather sorry for you. But the day I walked into my office in Santiago, and saw you rise to your feet and hold out your hand to me, I could not take my eyes off you, and you did your best to ignore me.'

'I was sure you must be married to Maria, and, knowing what I knew, I felt rather sorry for you, and didn't dare look at you.'

An arrested expression crossed his dark features. 'You felt sorry for me!' he exclaimed. 'I don't think anyone has felt sorry for me in my life, and I'm not sure I like the idea.'

'Don't worry.' Jules planted a kiss on his lips. 'I quickly got over it and quite a few times thought boiling in oil would be too good for you.'

Rand groaned. 'When I think how I behaved I don't blame you, but you fascinated and confused me so much I couldn't think straight. I had no intention of going through with a marriage of convenience, but when you turned *me* down, I found myself asking you again and again, the words just fell from my mouth in the heat of the moment. I think I knew then that I loved you, but I was too frightened to admit it even to myself.'

Jules had wondered, but she stopped wondering as they made slow, tactile love to each other, glorying in the intensity of sensations their openly confessed love for each other aroused, transporting them into a new dimension where they existed as one.

Nothing could go wrong now, surely, Jules thought, looking anxiously out of the living-room window. Friends and family had been arriving for the past two days: Sanchez and Donna with their new baby, Ester and Tony and friends of Rand's from all over the globe. It was a glorious summer day, her wedding day. Tina, her bridesmaid, had left for the church half an hour ago.

Jules swung back to her mother. 'Are you sure the bridal car was booked for two? I know the bride is supposed to be fashionably late, but that does not apply to the car. It is almost twenty past.'

Liz, resplendently dressed in a mauve silk suit and huge hat, as befitted the mother of the bride, smiled at her daughter with tears in her eyes. Jules had never looked more beautiful, in a classic-cut white satin gown embroidered in tiny crystals around the sweetheart neckline and short sleeves. The skirt followed the contours of her body and flared out at the back in an elegant train, also crystal encrusted. Her magnificent hair was a tumbling mass of curls, left loose on the strict instructions of Rand, and a crystal tiara supported the delicate veil.

'Mother, stop going all misty. What are we going to do?'

A knock at the door and the problem was solved and five minutes later her mother murmured, 'We have arrived, darling.'

As mother and daughter alighted from the bridal car at the gate of Chipping Beecham's ancient parish church, a great cheer went up as almost the whole town had turned out for what was without doubt the wedding of the year.

Jules smiled at all the grinning faces as she walked up the path. Tina was waiting and quickly adjusted her veil and the train of her gown, before she walked into the church on her mother's arm.

But once in the church the bride had eyes for no one but the tall, dark and incredibly handsome groom standing by the altar waiting for her...

Everyone agreed it was a very moving service and when the priest said, 'You may kiss the bride,' a collective sigh went up at the beauty of the moment, that eventually as the kiss went on turned to laughter, and that woke the youngest member of the congregation, Donna's son, and made him cry.

But by the time the noise registered with Jules she was walking back down the aisle married to the man of her dreams and too happy to care…

# MILLS & BOON® PUBLISH EIGHT LARGE PRINT TITLES A MONTH. THESE ARE THE EIGHT TITLES FOR JUNE 2004

❦

## SOLD TO THE SHEIKH
Miranda Lee

## HIS INHERITED BRIDE
Jacqueline Baird

## THE BEDROOM BARTER
Sara Craven

## THE SICILIAN SURRENDER
Sandra Marton

## PART-TIME FIANCÉ
Leigh Michaels

## BRIDE OF CONVENIENCE
Susan Fox

## HER BOSS'S BABY PLAN
Jessica Hart

## ASSIGNMENT: MARRIAGE
Jodi Dawson

MILLS & BOON®

*Live the emotion*

0504 Rom LP

# MILLS & BOON® PUBLISH EIGHT LARGE PRINT TITLES A MONTH. THESE ARE THE EIGHT TITLES FOR JULY 2004

---❦---

## THE BANKER'S CONVENIENT WIFE
Lynne Graham

## THE RODRIGUES PREGNANCY
Anne Mather

## THE DESERT PRINCE'S MISTRESS
Sharon Kendrick

## THE UNWILLING MISTRESS
Carole Mortimer

## HER BOSS'S MARRIAGE AGENDA
Jessica Steele

## RAFAEL'S CONVENIENT PROPOSAL
Rebecca Winters

## A FAMILY OF HIS OWN
Liz Fielding

## THE TYCOON'S DATING DEAL
Nicola Marsh

MILLS & BOON®

*Live the emotion*